VERMIN

WILLIAM A. GRAHAM

BLACK & WHITE PUBLISHING

First published 2018
by Black & White Publishing Ltd
Nautical House, 104 Commercial Street
Edinburgh EH6 6NF

1 3 5 7 9 10 8 6 4 2   18 19 20 21

ISBN: 978 1 78530 198 8

A CIP catalogue record for this book is available
from the British Library.

Typeset by Iolaire, Newtonmore
Printed and bound by CPI Group (UK) Ltd. Croydon, CR0 4YY

For Helen ... and Elaine, Johnnie and Willie.
But mostly for Helen.

Prologue

Henry Lewis MP raised his left buttock just a few millimetres off the green leather bench and farted gently. On
this particular occasion he wasn't in the House, though he
had passed wind in the Palace of Westminster more than
once and had received some disapproving looks from his
colleagues. No, this time he was dining in a very expensive
Italian restaurant in Soho and had just guzzled a huge plate
of chicken covered in a creamy sauce. Henry couldn't be
bothered trying to pronounce the name of the dish when
he ordered. He loved Italian food but, frankly, he couldn't
be arsed with menus printed in the language, so he had just
pointed to it. And he had told the waiter not to bring any
vegetables, but he could manage a side order of chips.

Henry glanced at his two dining companions, but if they
had noticed the fart they were keeping it to themselves; he
thought the one on the left had wrinkled his nose slightly,
but it was so bloody dark in the restaurant he couldn't be
sure. Anyway, even if they had, they weren't going to say
anything. They wanted something from Henry. Only, the
poor fools didn't realise it was highly unlikely he could
deliver it.

Jamie and Adrian worked for one of the biggest online

betting companies in the UK. They had invited Henry to dinner and Henry knew why, even though it had taken them until the main course was served to get round to discussing it. The online betting industry was booming and the Chancellor was looking for a bigger piece of the action. Jamie and Adrian's employers didn't want to pay any more tax than they had to – in fact, they didn't want to pay any at all. So they had suggested that Henry ask a question in the House, pointing out that the online betting industry had been one of the major success stories in recent years, how it had contributed hugely to the Treasury and how many people it employed. Wouldn't it be a pity to put all that at risk by burdening the industry with more taxes?

Henry could hardly refuse their invitation. For a start, he did owe them a four-figure sum. And he would try to raise the matter in the House, but the chances of that happening were about as good as one of the donkeys he bet on coming in at a hundred to one. It had been a long time since anyone had paid any attention to Henry, and that wasn't going to change any time soon.

When Henry had entered parliament sixteen years ago he had been keen to work his way up the greasy pole. Not to the very top, of course. Maybe not even to one of the great offices of state, although that would have been nice. But something like sport, or the arts or – God forbid! – Wales, even though he wasn't Welsh. Henry had ambition, but he was lazy. Not that that had stopped politicians in the past. Unfortunately, he also lacked any real talent. As the years passed and it became obvious that he was never going to get off the backbenches, Henry grew bitter. The whips had heard his whingeing in the bars, usually after a few too many glasses of wine, and they knew about his gambling.

Nothing much got past those bastards. Although, there was one little secret even they didn't know about.

Henry looked at the bottle of Barolo on the table. 'Not going to finish that?'

Jamie and Adrian smiled and shook their heads. In truth, Henry had drunk most of it.

'No point in letting it go to waste then.' Henry poured the last of the wine into his glass.

'Can we interest you in pudding?' asked Adrian – or was that Jamie? Henry was starting to forget who was who now.

He swallowed the dregs of his drink, wiped his mouth with his napkin and smiled blearily. 'Thanks lads, but I have to get back to my office. Few things I have to check before I can call it a night. Thanks for the meal. I'll do my very best to be of service to you. Now I must bid you goodnight.' He rose with the exaggerated care of someone who has had a lot to drink, and weaved towards the door.

As he walked out into the night, he smiled to himself. He was going to finish the night with dessert all right, but it wasn't going to come off the sweet trolley.

He walked to the end of the street and turned the corner. There weren't any expensive restaurants in this part of Soho, but at the next alleyway there was a small cafe. Henry had been there before and he knew he would find what he was looking for.

He looked through the window. There were only a few customers, sitting at tables with cups of coffee in front of them. None of them were eating and all of them were young men. Henry spotted one he hadn't seen before. He was slim and had blond curly hair, worn quite long. Henry felt the familiar stirrings. He rapped on the glass and all the boys turned their faces to the window. Henry pointed to the blond boy.

3

Seconds later, the boy stood facing him on the pavement. Close up, Henry could see that he was in need of a good wash. A change of clothes wouldn't go amiss either. He smelled like he hadn't changed for weeks. This didn't bother Henry. He knew there were places he could go where he could be entertained in nice flats by perfumed youths, but there were risks attached to those places. He didn't want some rent boy recognising him and selling him out to the papers. Even a backbench nobody like him would be worth a few grand.

The boy forced a smile. His eyes were dull – the result of banned substances, no doubt. He wouldn't even recognise his own mother. 'Forty for a blow job,' he said. Henry thought he could detect the trace of an accent. He wasn't surprised. These kids came from all over, thinking they could make it in the big city. Some went home. A lot ended up like this one, selling himself on the street. 'Or I can make it a wank for twenty.'

'In your dreams, sonny,' said Henry. 'I'll give you a tenner for that nice mouth of yours. I'll maybe make it twenty if you do a good job, or should I say *blow* job.' Henry smirked at his little joke. He knew just by looking that the boy needed the cash for his next fix. Negotiations were over.

The boy led Henry down the alleyway to a darkened doorway, then knelt and unzipped Henry's trousers. Henry's eyes closed in anticipation.

Then a voice said, 'That's far enough, son. You're coming with me.'

Henry opened his eyes and looked round. The man who had interrupted his moment of pleasure didn't look all that threatening, and he had spoken in a pleasant tone. 'You'll have to wait your turn, pal,' Henry said. 'Blondie and I have business to attend to.'

'Not tonight,' said the stranger. 'The boy's coming with me.'

Now Henry turned to face the man. He could be reasoned with, surely. 'You can fuck off, pal,' reasoned Henry, 'if you know what's –'

Pain exploded in Henry's gut. He hadn't seen the punch coming. The man had just seemed to lean forward, then straighten up. Henry bent over and began to retch. Creamy chicken, then Barolo. The boy sprang to his feet just in time to avoid the stream.

The man leaned over Henry and said, in the same reasonable tone, 'This is your lucky night. I know who you are. If I took a few pictures on my phone, then went to the papers, what's left of your career would be over. But that's not why I'm here. You have a wife and kids. Don't do anything like this again, because you'll get caught.'

The man took the boy's arm and led him away. Henry heard him say, 'Come on, Davie. We're going home.'

1

The sign on the door of my office says 'Allan Linton and Associates, Inquiry Agents'. That's not entirely accurate ... There is only one associate, and I don't pay him very much, or even very often, but I think 'Associates' sounds better and, who knows, maybe one day business will boom and I will have to go on a hiring spree. But, to be honest, that's not going to happen any day soon; not where I do my inquiring, here in Dundee. It's not exactly Los Angeles or New York – or even Glasgow.

When I tell people what I do for a living, the reactions are pretty much always the same. 'You're taking the piss, right?' Or a variation thereof. Then, in somewhat sceptical tones, they add, 'Are you like one of those private eyes on the telly, solving crimes and catching bad guys?'

The answer to both questions is, essentially, no. There is enough work, even in Dundee, for me to make a reasonable living, but I haven't really solved any crimes and, though I do know some people who could be described as bad guys, I've never caught any of them. I leave that kind of stuff to the boys in Bell Street, the local headquarters of Police Scotland.

Most of the time I find people: people who owe other people money, people whose families don't know where they are. I find them and I pass on the information that they are all right, or sometimes dead. I don't tell the families where to find their missing relatives, or lovers, etc. Most of the missing people have a very good reason for buggering off in the first place. It's up to them if they want to get back in contact.

On a few occasions, law firms have hired me to find an heir. One guy inherited over two hundred grand from some cousin he had never heard of. He couldn't believe it. He blew the lot on drugs. Until his windfall all he could afford was some weed at the weekend. Three months later, he died with a needle in his arm. Some guys have all the luck.

The nearest I got to actually catching a bad guy was when I was hired by one of Dundee's major pub chains. They have a big barn of a place in the city centre. They were selling a lot of alcohol, but the cash finding its way into the tills didn't match the sales. So I was 'employed' as a barman. After a month I reported back to the director who had hired me. When he asked which member of staff was stealing, I replied, 'All of them, except the manager.' The director didn't involve the police, but he sacked all of the staff, then the manager, for not seeing what was going on under his nose. Mind you, the manager was distracted by a pretty blonde barmaid who seemed incapable of fastening the top buttons of her uniform. All part of the thieves' plan, I reckoned. I picked up a decent fee for that little job, and I learned how to pull a proper pint.

The other question I'm often asked is: how do you become a private detective? Strangely enough, I haven't a clue. Sorry. Couldn't resist that. I'm fairly sure you can't do a degree in detecting, though I'm equally sure some enterprising university will get round to it sooner or later. You can get a degree in just about everything else these days. I think quite a lot of ex-coppers go into the private sector. Well, they have to augment their pitiful pensions somehow.

Actually, I was asked if I wanted to be a private detective. Simple as that.

Up till four years ago, I was the crime reporter at the local morning paper in Dundee. I thought I was doing a pretty good job, with a byline every week or so – not too bad when you consider that Dundee isn't exactly the crime capital of Scotland. Oh, we have plenty of crimes being committed, but it is usually pretty low-level stuff, with the odd murder thrown in every now and again.

Then two things happened: the old chairman of the company that owned the paper died, followed by my editor taking early retirement. The new guys who took over decided to modernise, which is a euphemism for sacking staff. To do this, they had to set up a human resources department. In the past, we'd had a personnel officer who looked after everything. Now, we had HR people – lots of HR people. That was the bit I couldn't understand: the company was taking on extra staff so that they could get rid of the people who were actually working there.

The end for me came when I had a performance appraisal with a young woman from HR. She looked up from her notes and said, very seriously, that I was absent from my desk for long periods. Equally seriously, I explained that I was a reporter and that stories didn't just land on my desk; I had to go out and speak to people. That seemed to puzzle her. Couldn't those people come into the office and speak to me? I had a hard enough job persuading some of those guys to meet me in the pub, even with the promise of free drink. I said, 'You've never worked in the newspaper business before, have you?'

She said that she had previously worked in HR for a double-glazing firm, but she didn't see how that was relevant. That's when I smiled, said she could stick her appraisal up her backside and walked out. Actually, I didn't say backside; I used another noun derived from the Anglo-Saxon.

Just as I thought, my new editor refused to back me up. The head of the HR department said that if I apologised to my appraiser they would review my position as a news gatherer. I said I was a reporter, not a news gatherer, and that I was going to have a word with my old school pal George, who was now a lawyer specialising in employment law. I can still see the grin on George's face when I went to see him. 'I've been waiting ages to have a go at those bastards,' he said wolfishly.

It never came to that. Newspapers like to report the news. They don't like making it. George sent them a letter, which mentioned tribunals more than once, and the next day I was offered a chunk of cash if I left quietly. So, I did. George was a bit disappointed. He'd been looking forward to his day in court, but I just wanted out.

The trouble was, it wasn't a very big chunk of cash, so I had to find another job pretty quickly and the only vacancy in Dundee for a crime reporter – sorry, *news gatherer* – was the one I had just created.

I considered a career change and finally came to a decision: I decided to go to the pub. I was just leaving my flat when my phone rang. A husky voice said, 'Hi, Allan. I need to see you.' Sadly, the voice didn't belong to some sultry temptress. My caller was a man in his late fifties, and the husky voice was the result of too many cigarettes.

I said, 'You're in luck, Eddie. I have the rest of the day free.' What started as a chuckle ended with a cough, and Eddie asked me to come to his office.

10

I'd first come across Eddie McLaren a few years back, when he was a witness in a trial I was covering. Eddie was a private detective. He'd been hired by a woman who suspected that her husband was having an affair. Eddie followed the guy to a house just outside Dundee, but the man didn't meet his lover there. Instead, he did a bit of breaking and entering. As he explained at the trial, he needed the extra cash to keep his wife in the manner to which she had become accustomed. Even the procurator fiscal had to smile.

Eddie and I met for a coffee after the trial. He was an easy guy to like. We swapped stories about Dundee's inept criminals and agreed to keep in touch. Which we did, every few months or so.

Eddie's office was on the top floor of a building in the centre of town. I knocked and went in. He didn't get up from his desk and waved me to the visitor's chair. He got right to the point. 'I hear you're unemployed.'

I smiled and said, 'That's right. Know anyone who's looking for a crime reporter?' Then it dawned on me. 'Don't tell me you're offering me a job? I didn't realise business was so good.'

Eddie looked at me – sadly, I thought – and said, 'It isn't, but I am offering you a job – mine.'

'You're retiring? But you aren't even sixty. Wait a minute. Have you won the lottery? Eddie, you sly –'

Eddie held up a hand and said, 'The very opposite, Allan, old pal. Cancer of the throat. The docs say I have three months at most.'

I suppose I shouldn't have been surprised; Eddie once told me he had started smoking when he was twelve and hadn't stopped since. I didn't think there was much point in saying anything to Eddie's news So, I didn't. Instead, I listened as he went on.

'I want you to take over the business, Allan. I've no one else to leave it to and I think you'd be good at it. You won't become rich, but I've made a decent living over the years. No reason why you can't do the same.'

Put like that, how could I refuse? So that's how I became a private investigator.

For the next few weeks, Eddie taught me everything he knew about the business, but then he went downhill rapidly. He didn't even make the three months. Just seven weeks after he offered me the job, he passed away in the kind of establishment no one ever comes out of, doped up to the eyeballs on morphine. The only people at his funeral were his lawyer and me.

2

It was just after ten on a Tuesday morning when there was a knock on the door of my office. Before I could say 'Enter', the door opened and standing there was a man aged about sixty. He looked around the room and decided not to make any comment; he probably wanted to spare my feelings. I would guess that his tie cost more than all the furniture put together.

'Mr Linton?' he asked. His accent was cultured and English.

'That's me,' I replied. I gestured to the client chair. He paused for a moment, taking a good look at it before he sat down, clearly resisting the urge to wipe it clean first.

'How can I help you?' I asked.

'I need you to find someone. I understand you have a talent for that.'

'That depends on who I'm looking for, and where I'm meant to be looking, Mr ... ?'

He hesitated, as if he couldn't remember his own name, then said, 'Carter, my name's Carter. I represent someone who wishes to remain nameless for the moment. My client is keen to establish the whereabouts of a young woman.'

'I'm pretty good at establishing whereabouts, but I'm going to need a bit more to go on, Mr Carter,' I said.

Carter looked a bit confused. I guessed this sort of thing was new to him. 'Ah, yes. Well, my client knew the young lady as Tina Lamont.' His brow furrowed. 'Though he surmises that may not be her real name. He met her in London, but she did tell him at one point that she came from here originally . . .' Carter hesitated again, this time as if he couldn't believe where he was. 'Here in Dundee. She may well have decided to return.'

'Which explains why you came to see me,' I said. 'You said you understood I had a talent for finding people, Mr Carter. Can I ask who told you that?'

'I know people here in the legal profession. That's all you need to know.'

'Actually, I need to know a lot more if you want me to take on this case,' I said. 'If I was writing all this down, the page would be blank.'

'I do have this,' said Carter. He reached into his jacket and pulled out a photograph, which he laid on my desk. I picked it up and studied it closely.

The girl in the photo wasn't drop-dead gorgeous, but she would definitely be worth a second look if you were sitting opposite her in the pub, even before your first drink. She was slim, with long straight blonde hair. And she was wearing a school uniform. That's not to say she was actually a schoolgirl. She could have been anywhere between fifteen and twenty-five. It's almost impossible to tell these days. Funny thing was, I know all the school uniforms in Dundee, and she wasn't wearing one of them.

Also, the photo didn't look posed, as all school photos do. She wasn't even looking at the camera. It looked like she had been unaware it was being taken. Perhaps it was taken on a phone.

14

I tapped the photo and looked up at Carter. 'If this is all you have, Mr Carter, then I doubt that I can help you.'

Carter reached once more into his jacket and pulled out a plain white envelope. He laid it out in front of me. 'There is £3000 in there, Mr Linton. That will be your retainer. There will be another £5000 on completion of your task. Of course, I'll meet any reasonable expenses. No need for receipts.'

They say money talks. Well, that three grand was howling in my ears. And I could hear the other five in the distance.

'I'm not going to make any promises, Mr Carter, but I'll do my best on your client's behalf. However, there's one thing I have to make clear: if I track down this young lady, I won't automatically tell you where she is. I'll tell her that you want to contact her, but then it'll be up to her if she wants to get in touch. I'll establish that she's well.'

'That's all we can ask, Mr Linton. I'll call you every few days for a report on your progress.'

'What if I have to contact you?' I asked.

Carter stood up, walked to the door and turned. 'That won't be necessary. As I said, I'll contact you. I must stress it's imperative that you keep this matter confidential, strictly confidential.'

Carter opened the door and almost walked straight into Niddrie, my aforementioned associate. The Englishman seemed to recoil, but quickly recovered his composure. Niddrie didn't even blink. Niddrie doesn't often blink.

'This is Niddrie, my associate. He'll be working with me on this investigation,' I said.

Carter examined my associate. I couldn't tell if he liked what he saw or not, but he said, 'Then I trust you'll stress to him the need for the utmost confidentiality.'

15

Niddrie stood aside and Carter started to move past him, but then stopped again and turned to face us.

'Oh, one more thing. I should have mentioned that, although she's a blonde in the photo, I know for a fact that Miss Lamont is a brunette.'

And with that intriguing snippet of information, the mysterious Mr Carter was gone.

3

Niddrie sat in the chair that Carter had just vacated. He'd sat in it lots of times over the last eighteen months without bothering to check it. Actually, Niddrie had been sitting when I first met him, on a bus heading into the city centre. My car was in for a minor repair, so I had decided to sample the delights of Dundee public transport.

The bus was almost empty. Apart from me, there was an elderly woman wearing a coat, even though it was what passes for a summer in Dundee, with grey hair sprayed rigidly into place. She sat at the rear of the bus. I was a few seats in front of her. There was also a man sitting near the front, though, if I have to be honest, I didn't really pay him any attention. At least, not at first.

Then this young guy got on. He was wearing a hoodie with a baseball cap underneath. Obviously, he was feeling the cold as much as the old dear, or maybe he was expecting rain. As he passed me on the way to the rear of the bus, I could see a short length of white wire leading up from the front of his top and disappearing underneath his hood. Judging by the racket as he passed, he hadn't been able to work out how to operate the volume control on the device secreted about his person. It sounded like someone grinding metal.

The young guy slumped down and put his feet on the seat opposite. I'm always a bit surprised that young guys like him spend a small fortune on trainers, but never seem to find the time to clean them.

The old lady looked over at him and tutted, but that had no effect. Her tut couldn't compete with the metal grinder. So, she tried glaring. That got the young guy's attention. 'Fuck are you looking at?' he inquired.

You had to give her credit. She wasn't backing down. 'Other people have to sit there. Why don't you put your mucky feet down? And turn the volume down as well. I don't want to have to sit here and listen to that awful racket.'

The hoodie guy leaned towards her and snarled, 'Then why don't you fuck off, you old cunt?'

I could see the old dear was shaken, and there was now a tremor in her voice when she said, 'You young hooligan. I'm going to report you'

'Why don't you shut your face before I shut it for you.'

At that point I thought I had to say something. Maybe the hoodie guy could be reasoned with. But before I could do anything, someone passed me on the way to the back of the bus. It was the guy I hadn't paid much attention to before. I now saw that he was wearing a green parka and he had blond hair, cut short.

He didn't seem in the least threatening when he leaned over the young guy. To be honest, he sounded almost concerned when he said, 'Here, son, playing that thing so loud could cause health problems.'

'Oh, yeah? You mean like fuck up my hearing?'

The young guy smirked. That was when the man grabbed the top edge of his hood and jerked it forward. He brought the young guy's face down hard on the edge of the back of the seat in front of him. I'm sure I heard something break, and it wasn't the seat.

The man yanked the hoodie guy's head back up. His face was a mess, blood dripping from his nose and mouth. The man leaned over and I strained to hear what he said.

'No, son, not your ears. I meant it could seriously damage your face.'

As the hoodie guy slumped back in the seat, his attacker looked round at me with deep green eyes. He didn't say anything, just raised an eyebrow. I smiled back and said, 'If I'd known it was going to be this much fun travelling by bus, I'd have bought a season ticket.'

Then I said, 'Might be a good idea to get off though. If someone calls the cops, you could end up being the one who gets arrested.' I turned to the old dear. 'Are you all right?' I needn't have asked. She beamed at her rescuer.

'Wait till I tell the girls at the bingo about this. This was better than winning a house.'

We rang the bell and walked to the front of the bus. A few seconds later, it stopped.

'I'll just get off here and get the next bus,' said the old lady. 'Good luck, lads, and thanks again.'

'We're getting off too,' I said to the driver, a small wiry woman.

'I'll call for an ambulance,' she said. She looked back at hoodie guy, who was still slumped on the seat, moaning. 'Silly laddie, but that's what you get when you don't stay in your seat on a moving bus. Just his bad luck I had to brake suddenly when that dog ran into the road.'

I pointed to the ceiling behind the driver. 'What about the CCTV?'

The driver grinned, 'Don't be daft. That thing doesn't

work. On you go, boys, hope to see you again soon. Remember – going by bus is the safest way to travel.'

As we walked away down the street, my old reporter's curiosity kicked in. I couldn't let this guy walk away without finding out more. So, I said, 'My name's Allan, Allan Linton. I could do with a drink after that traumatic experience. Can I buy you one?'

'Niddrie,' he said. No first name, no title. Not even doctor or professor. Just Niddrie.

He shook my hand. His grip was firm, like that of an old friend. 'That would be fine. I was on my way to the library, but there's no rush.'

Maybe he was going to take out a book on how to rescue damsels in distress on a Dundee bus. On second thoughts, maybe he'd already read it.

Dundee used to have a lot of pubs; some were full of character, some were full of characters, and some even had both. Over the years many had to close their doors, due in part to the urban vandalism passed off as the 'regeneration' of the city, but also because of a lack of customers. And characters in pubs seem to be a dying breed. I suspect the ones who are left prefer supermarket prices and drink at home. I took Niddrie to my office local, the Wig and Gown. It is in a building dating back to the end of the nineteenth century, close to the court buildings and police headquarters and surrounded by solicitors' offices. The clientele can easily afford to drink there. There may be some lawyers out there on minimum wage, but I've never met any.

I like the WAG, as it is known to its regulars. See, lawyers do have a sense of humour. Well, not all of them, but more about my ex-father-in-law later. The WAG has a magnificent gantry, a proper wooden bar, comfortable

seating and no noise except the quiet murmur of – mainly
– intelligent conversation. The sign over the door declares
it sells real ales and fine wines, and it keeps that promise.
I don't drink whisky, but friends who do assure me that
the selection on offer bears comparison with any pub in
Scotland, which means the world. If a stranger walked into
the bar, he would be convinced it hadn't changed since the
Victorian times.

The thing is, the WAG didn't exist until about ten years
ago. Before then, it was the ground floor of a large insurance
company, which moved to Perth when it was taken over by
an even bigger company. The gantry and bar are certainly
over a hundred years old, but they came from a pub that
was being demolished in Forfar.

When we walked in, I'm sure I saw a nod of approval
from Niddrie. 'Never been in here before,' he said. 'When
did it open?'

I told him and he said, 'I've been away for a while.'

We were served by the owner, Sandy Brackenridge. I first
met Sandy when he was a Detective Sergeant in Tayside
Police. We were never what you would call friends, but over
the years we had built up a healthy respect for each other.
He knew he could tell me things and be certain that they
wouldn't appear in print until he said so. In return, I had
passed on snippets of information I had picked up, which
often led to arrests. I noticed that Sandy took a good long
look at Niddrie as he pulled the pints.

Sandy used to tell me that, even as pubs were closing in
the centre of town, he was sure there was a market for a
decent bar in the right location. He took early retirement
when, as he put it, PC stopped meaning Police Constable
and started meaning 'politically correct'. His timing was

perfect; the insurance company premises had just become vacant and he knew all about the bar being demolished in Forfar. He had first seen it when he arrested a fence buying stolen credit cards there. He put the two together and came up with – in my opinion – what a pub should be.

Niddrie and I took our beers to a quiet corner and sat down. During my time as a crime reporter, I'd met some guys who thought they were hard men, and even one or two who really were hard men. Niddrie had just demonstrated how violent he could be, but he didn't feel the need to show it all the time. As far as I was concerned, he was one of the good guys.

Over the next hour or so I told him a lot about me and he told me almost nothing about himself. He had come back to Dundee after he retired. When I raised my eyebrows at this, and asked if he had found the secret of eternal youth – he barely looked forty – he said he'd been in the army. I asked which of Scotland's many fine regiments he served in. He took a sip of ale, looked me straight in the eye and said, 'The Pay Corps.'

I'd been a reporter for long enough to know it was time to stop probing, so instead we started talking about what I did for a living. When I told him, I swear he smiled. I was to find out that Niddrie wasn't big on displaying emotion. 'That sounds like it could be really interesting,' he said.

When we parted, Niddrie said, 'I enjoyed that. Maybe we could meet up again.'

I said that I would like that. I wouldn't say our friendship blossomed over the following months, because that implies it started small and grew. It wasn't like that. We just felt comfortable in each other's company from the start.

Some people might find our friendship unusual. I've

never found out what Niddrie's first name is. Honestly, it has never seemed to matter. And I've never found out where he lives, although I gathered that he had inherited a house in Dundee from his parents. I am able to contact him by calling his mobile. It's not exactly state of the art. In fact, I believe he has turned down offers from the antiquities sections of several museums for it, but, as Niddrie says, it's a bloody phone. He can turn on the oven himself when he gets home.

Niddrie knew where to find me and he took to dropping by my office. He liked talking about cases I was working on, and I found it useful to bounce ideas and theories off him. Before long, he was helping me out when I needed an extra pair of hands, or legs, or eyes. And that's when I added "Associates" to the sign on my door. He said he wasn't all that bothered about being paid – the perfect employee, or what? But, when I could, I passed on a percentage of the fee.

Now, sitting in my office, Niddrie looked at me and asked, 'What was that all about?' He didn't interrupt when I told him about our new commission from Mr Carter, not even when I mentioned the retainer. I finished, and finally he responded, 'So, we are looking for a girl whose real name we don't know, who may be aged anywhere between fifteen and twenty-five, and who may not even be in Dundee. Could be a tricky one.'

'The one thing we do know is that she's a brunette. But if Carter's acting for someone else, how come he knows that?'

4

Niddrie looked at the photo Carter had left. 'I suppose we could get lots of copies made and stick them on lamp posts with a contact number,' he said. 'You know, like people do with missing cats.' His cheek muscles seemed to ripple. Over time I've come to realise that's what passes for a smile for him. He always does that at his own jokes. It can be bloody irritating.

'That's a bit too low tech,' I said. 'Even for us. And I don't think our client would describe it as strictly confidential. Carter said that his client thought that Tina Lamont may not be the girl's real name, but let's suppose for a moment that it is – or a variation of it, like Christine or Christina. I can search the electoral roll.'

Actually, there were a few databases Eddie had told me about. I could try them, but I wasn't hopeful. You usually needed a bit more information than we had to make progress. Computers aren't the answer to everything.

Niddrie picked up the photo. 'I'll get one copy made for myself,' he said. 'I've had an idea. This Tina, whatever her name is, we know roughly how old she is, right? And what do girls of that age usually do at the weekends?'

'No need to be too graphic, Niddrie,' I said.

He shook his head. 'No, before they start all that stuff. They go to pubs and clubs, don't they? I could show the photo to the guys who work on the doors. Even if they haven't seen her before now, I could ask them to keep an eye out for her. I'll make up some story about her being my sister.'

'Think they'll do that?' I asked.

'They will if they think there's a few quid in it for them.'

'Worth a try,' I said. 'I'll make you a copy now.'

Niddrie stood up. 'Then I'll get going. I'm just off to the library.'

I made the copy and Niddrie put it in his inside pocket and left, leaving me mystified. Not about the case though – more about why he seemed to visit the library so often. I thought, I'm a detective; maybe I should investigate. But that would have to wait. First, I had to find Tina.

I spent the next few hours trawling through the databases but, as I thought, it was hopeless. I did find one Christine Lamont, but she turned out to be in her sixties.

I had decided to call it a day when the door of my office opened for the third time that day. It was a teenage girl wearing a school uniform, but it wasn't the elusive Miss Lamont, who had miraculously heard that I was looking for her. This girl's name was Ailsa, she was wearing the uniform of the local fee-paying school, and she was my daughter.

I'd met Ailsa's mum, Hannah, shortly after I became a crime reporter. She had just qualified as a lawyer and started work with one of Dundee's biggest law firms: McKendrick, Petrie and Clayton. It didn't hurt that Hannah's maiden name was McKendrick, but that wasn't the reason her dad had given her the job. Fergus McKendrick wasn't stupid.

His daughter was one of the brightest young legal prospects in Scotland and he didn't want her working for anyone else. And Fergus was a man used to getting his own way.

I'd been having a pint after work with my lawyer pal, George, when Fergus swept into the pub followed by a flock of underlings from his firm. Fergus didn't stop to say hello to George, so none of the rest of them did. Flock is the collective noun for sheep. George and Fergus were both lawyers, but that was about all they had in common. George had been brought up on the same housing estate as me. The McKendrick family home was a mansion built in the nineteenth century by one of the millionaires who had made his fortune in jute.

I had watched both in court; Fergus was a performer who turned his trials into theatre, whereas George was a street fighter. Another lawyer described him as a 'mean bastard'. When I told George, he grinned and said, 'I love it when I get a compliment from my peers.' Fergus and George's success rates in court were roughly equal, but I knew which one I'd want to represent me.

I felt the draught behind me as the door of the pub opened again. A moment later, a young woman joined us at the bar. She was slim, with short brown hair. I'd be willing to bet she hadn't bought her suit and shirt in the local branch of that well-known high street store – the one that uses highly paid supermodels in their TV ads when you know they wouldn't be caught dead shopping there. Her clothes were made for her and she was made to wear them. A hint of expensive scent wafted between us. I hadn't known that old George knew women like her.

'Hi, George,' she said. 'That was a smart piece of work, getting that young lassie off the other day.'

'Yeah, well, she was innocent of everything, except being conned into passing dud cheques by that prat of a boyfriend of hers.' George smiled.

She turned to me and raised a perfect eyebrow. George said, 'This is Allan, an old pal of mine. He's the crime reporter for the local rag.'

'I thought I had seen you before,' she said. And that's when I first noticed the twinkle in her eye.

Then a voice boomed across the room, 'Hannah! Where have you been? Come and join us.'

Hannah smiled and said, 'Sorry, got to go. Father calls.' She lingered for just a moment and added, 'Nice to meet you, Allan.'

I watched her walk across the room to be swallowed up by McKendrick and his flock. George nudged me and said, 'Forget it, Linton. She's way out of your league.'

But I couldn't forget that twinkle. I tried calling her office a couple of times, but she was always unavailable. So, I decided to go for a more subtle approach. I started hanging around the court building until I finally 'accidentally' bumped into her. The subtle approach . . . works every time.

Before I could make some pathetic attempt to ask her for a coffee or a drink, she said, 'Allan, hi! It's so nice to see you again. Hey, I was just going for a coffee. Care to join me?'

As we walked down the street she said, 'Actually, I thought that after George introduced us you might call me. You can always reach me through my office.' She turned to look up into my face, and there was that twinkle again.

When it comes to coffee shops, Dundee isn't exactly Seattle. Not that I've ever been there, but I've watched the reruns of *Frasier*. That said, there are a couple of places where you can sit in comfortable surroundings and be fairly sure that the stuff you are drinking didn't come out of a large catering can. Plus, you know you aren't contributing to the untaxed profits of large American companies.

For the next hour, we sat and talked. I'd never had a crush on a girl before, even when I was at school, but I had one then. Looking back, I'm pretty sure I could feel my skin tingling as I sat and listened to her describing the finer details of . . . Well, I can't remember what she was describing, but I can remember the tingling sensation. Be honest, there's no feeling quite like it.

I was about to ask if she wanted another coffee, when she looked at her watch and jumped to her feet.

'Oh, my God! Look at the time! I should've been home ages ago. Got to go.'

Before I could stand up, she was making for the door. She glanced back at me and grinned. 'Call me at the office. I'll tell my secretary to put you through next time.'

I decided to play it cool and waited till two minutes past nine the next day before I called her office again.

She came on the line and said seriously, 'Obviously you weren't in any hurry to get in touch. I've been at my desk since eight.'

I started to stutter that I would have called earlier when she laughed. 'Allan, I'm just teasing. So, where are you taking me tonight?'

God, that girl had mastered the art of catching you off guard. Where did you take Fergus McKendrick's daughter on a first date? It had to be somewhere special, somewhere expensive. The kind of place I never went to. I finally remembered a restaurant that George had told me about. He hadn't picked up the cheque; a grateful client had done that, much to his relief.

But when I suggested the name, Hannah snorted. 'Oh, God, no. Been there. Overpriced and the food has been rubbish since the previous chef walked out after a fight with one of the waiters. Lovers' tiff, so I heard. Actually, I fancy a few pints. You live in the Ferry, don't you? Lots of good pubs with good beers there. Meet you in The Ship at eight?'

Broughty Ferry was once a fishing village east of Dundee but over the years it was absorbed into the city. Dundonians think of it as a suburb, but Ferry folk think of themselves as a breed apart. There are no fishing boats any more, but the Ferry has a lot of pubs and one of the best is The Ship. It sits right on the waterfront, just a few yards from the old lifeboat station. You can look out of the windows and watch seals and porpoises in the River Tay.

My dad once told me that back in the seventies, one of Scotland's biggest brewers featured the pub in an ad campaign. The ad showed the American singer Bing Crosby sitting at the bar with a glass of lager. The bar, with its magnificent dark wood gantry, is unchanged, according to my dad, but no one has seen Mr Crosby there for a while. Maybe he didn't like the lager. No problem, the pub offers some excellent ales.

Even though my flat was only three minutes' walk from The Ship, I thought it best to make sure I wasn't late, although I also didn't want to look too keen. So, I waited till seven o'clock before I walked in.

I decided it wasn't a good idea to start drinking beer before Hannah arrived, so I ordered a mineral water and nursed it for the next hour and thirteen minutes. At one point the barmaid came over and asked if she should send for the paramedics. There was obviously something seriously wrong with me. Hah! I'd show her. No tip for her tonight.

I had my back to the door when I heard it open. I didn't need to turn round to know it was Hannah. Every man in the bar was looking that way, most with their glasses paused halfway to their lips.

I turned and there she was, in faded jeans, ankle boots and a man's shirt, with a sweater draped over her shoulders. Was there anything this girl couldn't wear? She walked over and kissed me on the cheek. I heard a collective sigh around the bar. Boy, did I feel good!

'Sorry, I had to wait for a taxi. You haven't been waiting long have you?'

'Oh, no, just got here,' I said nonchalantly. 'Haven't even had time to order a beer.'

The barmaid whisked away the almost empty glass of water. She smiled sarcastically at me. 'You won't be wanting this any more then.' She turned to Hannah and smiled again, this time without the sarcasm. 'What can I get you, young lady?'

'Is that Thrapple Dowser I see?' asked Hannah. 'A pint please, and the same for my wimpy friend.'

'Good choice,' said the barmaid, and set to pulling the pints.

We staggered out of the pub at closing time. To be completely accurate, I staggered. Hannah sort of glided out on to the street.

'I must insist on taking you home,' I said.

She looked at me. 'If you can take me as far as the taxi rank, it'll be a miracle.'

When we reached the rank, the driver took one look at me and said, 'No way he's coming in my cab.'

Hannah said, 'No, it's just me.' She looked at me. 'Are you going to get home all right, Allan?'

30

By good fortune, someone had had the foresight to put the taxi rank just outside the entry to my flat.

'Yes,' I said. 'I think I can manage that.'

Hannah reached up and kissed my cheek. 'That was what I call a first date.'

'If that was the first, does that mean there's going to be a second?' I asked.

Hannah got in the taxi, rolled down the window and said, 'This is the most fun I've had in ages. We're just getting started, Allan.'

Over the next few weeks we started seeing one another fairly regularly. We went to the pub and we talked more than we drank. I also took her to dinner a couple of times. Nothing fancy, but Dundee does have a few restaurants where you can eat well without having to pray that your credit card isn't going to be declined.

It was at the end of one of those meals that I happened to mention that my favourite film was on TV later that week.

'Oh, *Casablanca*!' Hannah grinned. 'I love that movie.'

'Come over and we can watch it together,' I said. 'I promise not to cry at the end if you don't.'

So, Hannah came over and we watched Bergmann and Bogart's doomed affair for the umpteenth time. My upper lip remained resolute, but when I turned to Hannah her eyes were glistening.

'Time for a coffee before you go?' I asked.

'Actually, I prefer tea with my breakfast,' she said.

'Does that mean what I think it means?'

'Oh, Allan,' she said, rolling her eyes. 'You're useless.' Then she looked serious and said, 'Well, I hope you're not useless where we're going now. Your bedroom's this way, isn't it?' She grabbed the front of my shirt and led the way.

To be honest, it was all a bit of a rush that first time. But I'm fairly sure she didn't think I was completely useless, because we did it all over again an hour or so later ... then once more just before we got up.

Hannah made for the shower and I stopped admiring her rear end long enough to say, 'I'd better make that tea now. I've kept you waiting long enough.'

She turned and the view got even better. 'No time. Got to go home and get changed. I'm due in the office in an hour.'

A couple of days later I was sitting at my desk when the chairman's secretary, Margaret, called me. 'The chairman wants to see you.'

Apart from the odd pleasantry exchanged while sharing the lift or passing in the corridor, I had never had a conversation with the old boy. As I headed to his office I wondered what I had done. Maybe I hadn't done anything. Maybe he wanted me to take over as managing editor. Maybe I had been just a little too inventive with my expenses last week. There wasn't much got past the old boy.

I knocked on the door of the outer office and went in. Margaret shook her head and looked at me sternly. 'You are to go straight in. What have you done, Mr Linton?'

The chairman gestured to the chair in front of his desk. He got straight to the point.

'I have had a telephone call from Mr Fergus McKendrick of McKendrick, Petrie and Clayton. I understand you know his daughter?'

I nodded, but before I could say anything, the old boy went on, 'Not to beat about the bush, but he wants this relationship to end immediately and he has asked me for my help to ensure that it does. His very words were, "If he doesn't do what he's told I want you to sack him."'

What a bastard, I thought. Well, it wasn't going to work. I opened my mouth to say 'In that case, I quit!' when the old boy held up a hand.

'I told him to fuck off,' he said in pretty much the same tone as he used when commenting on the weather during our occasional meetings in the lift. 'What you do in your own time is your business, as long as it doesn't reflect badly on the firm,' he continued. 'And courting a very pretty girl like Hannah McKendrick certainly does not do that.'

Then he smiled. 'You know, if I was forty years younger, you'd have some serious competition. There aren't many like Hannah – nothing like her father, thank God. Pompous old fart. Actually, I really enjoyed telling him where to go. Should have done it years ago.'

He laughed and we both stood. 'Well,' he said with a sigh. 'I suppose you've better things to do than listen to me rambling on. Off you go.'

As I passed Margaret's desk on my way out, she raised an eyebrow. 'It's okay,' I said. 'He didn't fire me.'

'Oh, I knew he wouldn't.' She smirked. 'You should've seen him when he came off the phone with McKendrick. I've never seen him look so pleased with himself.'

That evening I was sitting in my flat wondering if I should call Hannah and tell her about her father's request to the chairman, when the doorbell rang. Hannah stood in the doorway. I could tell that she had been crying, but I was pretty sure it wasn't because she had been watching *Casablanca* again. She looked furious. I also noticed that there was a large bag at her feet.

'I found out what Dad said to your boss,' she said. 'We

had a blazing row. I told him he had no right to do that. He said that as long as I was living under his roof I would do as he said. I told him no problem, I was leaving.'

There was a pause. Hannah lowered her eyes then looked up at me. 'But now I've nowhere to stay.'

'What a coincidence,' I said. 'I've just been sitting here thinking of advertising for a lodger. There will be strict conditions, of course. The successful applicant will need to clean the flat and cook dinner every night. And, of course, I would be in sole charge of the remote control.'

Hannah laid her head against my chest and sighed. 'Oh, Allan.' I thought that maybe I should also have stipulated that she did all my washing as well. She stepped back and looked up at me. There was that bloody twinkle again. 'In your dreams. Bring my bag in. And you might as well cancel your Sky Sports subscription. Now, let's order in a takeaway. I'll choose.'

I'd never lived with anyone before and, as it turned out, neither had Hannah. But, from the very start, we seemed to get it right. It was the best of times.

Then Hannah came home from work one day and said she had something to tell me. She was pregnant. We had talked about having children at some unspecified time in the future, but just not yet. We had been careful but, obviously, not careful enough.

'I'm going to keep the baby, Allan,' she said, and there was a determined look on her face.

It's a lot to take in when you are told you are going to be a father, especially when it's the last thing you were expecting to hear, so I didn't reply right away.

'Say something,' she said.

'You know what this means, don't you? No more Thrapple Dowser for you, young lady. At least till our son's born.'

34

She punched me in the chest and said, 'Who says it's going to be a boy?' She looked at me seriously again. 'Are you sure about this, Allan?'

'Well, I could see if there is a home for fallen women with vacancies,' I joked. 'Of course I'm sure.' Truth was, I was happier than the pig in the proverbial. We went to bed early that night.

The next morning, I brought Hannah her tea in bed. 'I've been thinking,' I said.

Hannah looked at me sternly. 'Never a good idea,' she replied.

I went down on one knee at the side of our bed and looked her in the eye. 'Hannah McKendrick, will you do me the great honour of agreeing to become my wife?'

Hannah looked back at me impishly. 'Why, Mr Linton, surely you should first ask my father if he will give his permission?'

'I think we both know what his answer would be, so we'll skip that part,' I said.

Hannah looked solemn. 'Allan, please don't think you have to do this.'

'I'm not asking because I think I have to,' I replied. 'I'm asking because I want to. Because I've wanted to since the day I met you and because I love you. I love you so much.'

A tear appeared in the corner of her eye. 'Oh, and I love you, Allan. Let's get married!'

Hannah's tea went cold and we were both late for work that morning.

A few weeks later, we were married in the small kirk that Hannah's mum attended. I think that Janette McKendrick had a lot to do with arranging it at such short notice. Fergus didn't come, of course. He had made it clear that he thought Hannah was marrying beneath her. My dad didn't come either, but at least he had a decent excuse. He had been living in Spain for the past seven years. He did send his best wishes, which was more than Fergus did.

'I did try to persuade him,' Janette whispered to me. 'But he can be such a stubborn old fool.'

I liked Hannah's mum. After the service, she said, 'Look after my daughter, Allan. That's all I ask.' I promised I would.

Seven months later, we welcomed Ailsa Janette Linton into the world. So, it wasn't a boy, but I couldn't have cared less. From the first moment the midwife in Ninewells Hospital held her up to me, I lost my heart to this tiny creature with a pink, scrunched-up face. She was perfect in every way. I thought life couldn't get any better. I was right. It didn't.

Hannah took her full maternity leave, and then announced she was going back to work. That didn't come as a surprise. She had talked of little else for weeks. Then came the question of who would look after our daughter. My mum wasn't around. In fact, I had no idea where she was. Hannah said she had spoken to Janette, and she was happy to take Ailsa during the day.

That seemed to work for a few weeks. Until one day I rang the doorbell of the McKendrick mansion and was greeted by a woman I had never seen before.

'I've come to collect Ailsa,' I said, confused.

'Of course,' said the woman. 'She's sleeping but I'll just fetch her. Please wait here.'

'Where's Mrs McKendrick?'

'She had to go out.' The woman went into the house and reappeared a minute later with Ailsa, who was fast asleep in her carrycot.

When Hannah got home that night I told her what happened and asked if she knew who the young woman was, and why her mother wasn't there looking after our daughter.

'Ah, yes, I've been meaning to talk to you about that,' she said. 'Mum has been feeling the strain a bit recently. Her doctor told her to take things easy, so we decided to bring in someone to help.'

I took a deep breath before asking, 'Don't you think you should have discussed it with me before you decided to hire a nanny?'

Hannah smiled at me. 'She's not a nanny. She just comes in during the day. After mum had seen the doctor we had to make a decision quickly. Look, Allan, everything's working out perfectly. Rosie, that's her name, used to look after the children of one of the lawyers in dad's firm. She comes highly recommended.'

'And how much is Rosie costing us?' I asked.

Hannah smiled again, a bit more tightly this time. 'Oh, you don't have to worry about that. We can afford it.'

I couldn't argue with that. Provincial journalists don't earn a fortune, but Hannah was probably earning more than twice what I was. Plus, I didn't want to put any more pressure on Janette.

'Okay,' I said, resigned. 'Let's see how it goes.'

Actually, it went really well. Rosie was very good at her job and she genuinely seemed to care for our daughter. Little Ailsa thrived under her care and I noticed that Janette looked a lot more relaxed.

Ailsa was just over a year old when we had to make our

next big decision, and this time Hannah did discuss it with me. We had to find a bigger house. We were still staying in my flat, but it had only the one bedroom. I had converted the large box room into a nursery for Ailsa, but that was always going to be a temporary solution. I agreed that we should start looking right away.

I thought we would just stay in the Ferry. I found a couple of properties I thought would suit us, but when we went to view them it was obvious from the beginning that Hannah wasn't interested.

Then she announced that she had found the perfect place. It was in the West End, a five-minute walk from her parents' house. Now, I didn't want to live any nearer to Fergus McKendrick than I had to, but I agreed to go and look at it.

There used to be several large estates to the west of Dundee, mainly owned by the guys who had built the huge jute mills. I once heard that there were more Rolls Royce cars per head of the population in Dundee than anywhere else in the world. Now, I don't know if that was true but there was a lot of money in the city in those days – although not everyone could afford a Roller. Those jute barons kept a very tight grip on their fortunes. The men and women they employed were paid a pittance. My late granddad had told me the stories of his parents, who had worked in the mills. They couldn't even afford to buy him a pair of roller skates.

The jute industry declined, then disappeared, and the big estates were swallowed up as the city expanded west. The land was used for building more modest houses. But many of the lodge houses, which had once stood at the entrances to the estates, survived. We went to see one of them.

Hannah was right. It was perfect. It retained a lot of its old

character, but the present owners had renovated it sympa-
thetically. It had a large enclosed garden at the rear. Before
we left, Hannah was already deciding where she would
put her furniture. I know when I'm beaten. And I'd done
my research. There were a couple of decent pubs within
reasonable walking distance.

Then we started talking money. I pointed out that even
with Hannah's salary, we were going to be stretched.
Hannah simply smiled. 'Oh, we don't have to worry about
a mortgage. I've arranged a loan from my firm at a very
reasonable rate of interest.'

I said, 'I thought we were going to discuss things like this
before we made any decisions.'

Hannah rolled her eyes. 'It's a no-brainer. Surely you see
that, Allan?' Then she put her head on my chest and said,
'And you love the house as much as I do, don't you?'

And so I gave in again.

We moved in a few weeks later. Rosie came in during the
week to look after Ailsa. After a couple of years, I started
dropping hints that Ailsa might like a little brother or sister,
but Hannah kept saying the time wasn't right. Her career
was going well and she was sure she was in line for a part-
nership very soon.

Janette doted on her granddaughter and, just before
Ailsa's fifth birthday, she said she would like to throw a
special party for her. Before I could reply she said, 'And I'd
like Fergus to be there.' I had had as little to do with the old
bugger as I could, but I did know that Ailsa meant a lot to
him. What could I say but yes?

The party was held at his house. There was more room
there to accommodate the hordes of yelling kids and their
cocktail-swigging mothers. The long drive was full of

BMWs and Mercs. I felt right at home. But Ailsa had a good time, which was all that mattered.

When the party was over, Ailsa fell asleep in my arms. We were just saying our goodbyes to Janette, when Fergus appeared with a large glass of brandy in his hand. It wasn't his first.

He beamed at Hannah. 'Good news. I've been meaning to tell you all day. I've had a word with a few people and Ailsa's been accepted at your old school. She'll start after the summer.'

Hannah had attended Dundee's fee-paying school. Now, I have nothing against private education. I've sat and yelled at leftie politicians on the telly telling me how unfair private schools are. They are the same bunch who attended such places themselves, then sent their own kids to those self-same schools. If they had gone to state schools, like I did, I might have been prepared to listen. Life is unfair and any advantage you can give your kid, you should grab. But I still didn't like Fergus McKendrick telling me he had chosen my kid's school.

'Thanks for your efforts, Fergus,' I said. 'But I'll decide which school Ailsa goes to.'

Fergus turned to me. He was swaying a bit now. 'If it's the fees you are worried about, you don't have to bother. I'll take care of them.'

I felt like hitting him. 'I don't need your charity. I can pay for my daughter's education myself.'

Fergus gave me a nasty grin. 'You weren't so high and mighty when I bought your house for you.'

I looked at Hannah.

'Dad, you fucking idiot,' she hissed.

Fergus looked around the room, an expression of fake innocence on his face. 'What? I thought everyone knew.'

'Hannah's right. You're a fucking idiot,' Janette snapped before turning and marching out of the room.

And that was it. We'd had the best of times. Now it was the worst of times.

I slept in the spare bedroom that night.

The next morning, Hannah said to me, 'You've every right to be angry with me. All I can say is I thought I was doing the right thing.'

'I'm not angry,' I replied. 'More sad than anything else. You did what you thought was right. It's just not the way I would've done it. We just want different things.'

'We've changed, Allan,' she said.

'You have, but I'm still the same. That's a problem I don't think we can solve.'

I looked her in the eye, but the twinkle wasn't there. I knew it was over. 'I'll go and stay with George until I can find a place,' I said.

We divorced quietly a few months later. George was commiserating with me in the pub when Fergus swept in with his entourage. He smiled triumphantly at me. I started to stand up, but George put his hand on my arm. 'Leave it,' he said. 'If it's any consolation, I hear that Hannah refuses to talk to him.'

There was some sort of custody arrangement worked out, but in practice I was able to see Ailsa pretty much any time I wanted. 'She's yours as much as mine,' Hannah told me.

Ailsa did take her place at her mum's old school. Hannah and I split the fees.

Now, ten years later, my daughter stood in front of me. 'Dad,' she said. 'I'm in trouble.'

5

Ailsa saw the look of horror on my face and rolled her eyes. She looked so much like her mother when she did that.

'No, not that kind of trouble.' She gave an exaggerated sigh and slumped into the chair recently vacated by Niddrie. 'I'm not an idiot.'

'Whatever you've done, I'm sure we can fix it,' I said.

'That's just it. I haven't done anything. There's this boy at school. His name's Scott. He's two years ahead of me. He keeps asking me out. I keep telling him no, but he doesn't stop. Now he's started telling all his friends that it's the other way round and that I fancy him.' Now my little girl looked thoroughly pissed off. 'But it's more than that. He's saying that we've had sex and that I'll do anything for him – you know, sex-wise.'

I suppressed a shudder. There are some things a father doesn't need to hear.

Ailsa went on, unabashed, 'He's the captain of the First XV and lots of girls fancy him, so everyone believes him.'

'A talented sportsman *and* a real arsehole. Such a rare combination,' I said. 'Have you spoken to your mother about this?'

Ailsa shook her head. 'I can't. This boy, Scott? His second name is Clayton.'

I nodded. 'He wouldn't be related to Malcolm Clayton, by any chance?'

Ailsa looked at me. 'He's his son.'

Now I knew why Ailsa hadn't spoken to her mother. Malcolm was the Clayton in McKendrick, Petrie and Clayton. I didn't know the family personally, but I did know that Scott was an only child and his parents thought the sun shone out of his backside. I could see that they might not be too happy being told that their blue-eyed boy was a lying toerag. That could cause problems in the firm of M, P and C.

'Leave it with me,' I said. 'I'm sure I can make Master Clayton see the error of his ways.'

Ailsa looked at me apprehensively. 'You aren't going to hit him or anything are you?' Then she looked thoughtful. 'Not that I would be against seeing that, mind you.'

I smiled at her. 'No, I'll try reasoning with him first. If that doesn't work, only then will I try the various forms of torture perfected by the Spanish Inquisition.'

Ailsa looked puzzled, 'The Spanish who?'

I shook my head. 'Good to know the fees I pay half of aren't being wasted. Have a word with your history teacher. Don't worry, honey. We'll sort it out.'

Ailsa came round my desk and hugged me. 'I know you will, Dad. You're the best.' And she skipped out of my office.

Whatever had happened between us, Hannah and I had got something right with our daughter. Maybe I would skip the reasoning part with that young prick and just go straight to the torture chamber after all.

The next morning, Niddrie came into the office and sat down. 'Any luck with the searches online?' he asked.

'Not so far,' I replied. 'In the meantime, there is something I want you to do for me.'

I told him about Ailsa's problem with Prince Charming. Niddrie didn't react, just sat there and listened.

'I want you to check him out,' I said. 'I'd do it, but he knows me. He doesn't know you.'

'No problem. It'd be useful if I had a photo of him though.'

'I thought of that.' I laid a copy of Ailsa's school magazine on my desk and opened it. Ailsa had got it for me because she was featured in the debating team.

But it wasn't her photo that I pointed out to Niddrie. It was the First XV rugby team. There in the middle was their captain, Scott Clayton. He was a big lad with a mop of blond hair. And he had a smug, arrogant expression, on a face that you would never get tired of punching. At least, I wouldn't.

Niddrie studied it for a few moments then nodded to himself. 'Okay, got it. I can't speak to the bouncers till the weekend, so I'll take a look at him today. What are you going to do about the mysterious Miss Lamont? More looking online?'

I shook my head. 'No, I think I'll take a break from that. But I've had an idea. What if it isn't just Mr Carter's client who wants to find her? What if the police are looking for her too, for instance? That could explain the fake name.'

'Could be,' mused Niddrie. 'But we can hardly show her photo to the boys in Bell Street and ask them. I don't think Mr Carter would think that was acting in the strictest confidence.'

'There is someone else I can ask. Michael Grant.'

'Want me to come with you?' Niddrie asked.

'No, I think it's better if I see him alone.'

'Fair enough,' said Niddrie, rising to his feet. 'Then I'll go and keep an eye on young Clayton.'

Michael didn't like surprise visits, so I called his mobile number. He was at home and he said he could see me. Ten minutes later I was in my car, heading out of the city.

I always have to laugh when I see private detectives on TV or in films driving some fancy car – some huge four-by-four or exotic sports car. I drive a small Korean hatchback. Eddie McLaren had always told me that a good investigator should be inconspicuous, if not downright invisible. People might notice a Ferrari, but they aren't going to pay too much attention to a Hyundai.

I turned on the CD player and, with perfect timing, there it was, Tony Hicks's chugging guitar in the opening sequence of 'I Can't Let Go', one of the greatest pop songs of all time by one of the greatest bands – the Hollies.

A lot of people think it's a bit strange that I love the music from a time long before I was born but, hey, I don't think that people who like Mozart are weird. The reason is simple: my dad. He was a drummer in a local band in the sixties. They were well known, mainly on the east coast of Scotland, and actually went full-time for a couple of years. But they never hit the big time. Dad said they were pretty good musicians but when everything went psychedelic towards the latter half of the decade, they decided to pack it in. As my old man said, 'No one was going to make me wear a bloody flower in my hair. I just wanted to play rock and roll.'

I grew up listening to the early Beatles, the Stones, the Who, etc. Strangely enough, my dad didn't have any Seekers or Engelbert Humperdinck albums. Then, when I was in my teens, he took me to see the Hollies playing the Caird Hall in Dundee. They still had three of the original band from the sixties – men in their fifties. You can keep all your manufactured boy bands. These guys could play and sing live. I was gripped by the music and it never let me go.

Michael Grant's house was to the north of Dundee. He had bought the land and had an architect design the house exactly as he wanted it. Michael tended to get things exactly as he wanted them. The house was a couple of miles off the main road to Forfar and enclosed by a high wall. I pulled up at the gates and told the intercom that I had arrived. It didn't bother to reply, but the gates swung open slowly and I started up the drive.

After about half a mile, I pulled up in front of the house. I'd been there before, but I still couldn't get over its contrast with the house that Michael grew up in. That was two doors down from my family's, in the sprawling housing estate called Fintry, just a half hour's drive back to the outskirts of Dundee. That entire house in Fintry could fit into Michael's present lounge, with room to spare. Michael Grant was my oldest friend . . . and Dundee's biggest drug dealer.

6

I'd been at primary school for a couple of years when Michael and his parents moved to our street. In those days, most of the dads went to work and most of the mums stayed at home and looked after the kids. It was the other way round in the Grant house. Michael's mum had at least a couple of jobs, but his dad stayed home – only I don't remember him looking after young Michael. Grant senior seemed to spend most of his day sprawled in front of the television, and only left the house to visit the local off-licence. He'd already been barred from the two local pubs.

I can still remember Miss Robertson, my teacher, introducing Michael to the class. He was wearing trousers that looked about two sizes too big and a woollen jersey with patches at the elbows. I learned later that his mother found his clothes in local charity shops, but she also made sure that he was spotlessly clean.

Kids can be such little arseholes and my class was no exception. The giggling and sniggering started right away. Michael glared defiantly back. Miss Robertson pretended not to notice and said, 'Now, who would like Michael to sit beside them?'

The sniggering got louder, then someone put their hand up . . .

'He can sit beside me,' I said. Seven years old and already the champion of the downtrodden.

That didn't mean Michael was overcome with gratitude. He glowered at me as he sat down and didn't say a word to me for the rest of the day. Looking back, I think he simply didn't trust anyone. Up till then, he hadn't found anyone he could trust.

The gigglers and the sniggerers continued to make fun of Michael. He was never invited to join in the games in the playground – not that it bothered him. I wasn't one for games either, so I used to spend free time in the small school library. I was the only one from our class who did. One day, when I saw him standing alone in the playground, I asked him if he'd like to come with me.

Now, I thought I wasn't a bad reader, but Michael was at least two years ahead of me. He devoured books. And now that we had a common interest, we actually started talking to one another.

Miss Robertson picked up on this and started to lend Michael books. Her heart was in the right place, but this just led to the other kids calling him the teacher's pet. He couldn't have cared less.

We were coming home one day when our path was blocked by a pack of the sniggerers, who had brought along a couple of big brothers as backup. They started pushing Michael, and one of the bigger boys grabbed one of his books and held it up so he couldn't reach it. I asked them to stop it but was told to keep out of it. Then Michael's face seemed to darken. He punched his tormentor in the gut then grabbed the book as it fell. The rest of the pack fell on him, pinning him to the ground.

The boy who had been punched drew back his foot to kick Michael in the ribs, but I rushed at him and sent him flying. Michael struggled to his feet and I went to his side. 'Come on then,' I said. So they did, and we got a bit of a hammering. Sometimes it can be hard going being a champion of the downtrodden. Eventually, they got fed up and left us.

As we limped home, I offered Michael my handkerchief to wipe his bloody nose. He never carried one. He looked at me and said, 'Why'd you do that? You could've got away.'

I grinned at him. 'Because that's what friends do, and we're friends, right?' And, for the first time, Michael smiled back at me.

Over the coming years there were more fights, and when I came home with cuts and bruises my mother would say, 'This never happened before that Grant boy came here. I want you to stay away from him. He's nothing but trouble.'

But then my dad would take me aside and say quietly, 'You do what you think is right, son. Pals stick up for each other.' Then he'd slip me some money and tell me to take Michael for some chips. 'That laddie always looks like he could do with feeding up,' he'd say.

As we got bigger, we started to win more fights than we lost, and the other kids began to leave us alone.

But Michael's home life didn't improve. I didn't see much of his mother; she left early for work and didn't come home till late. When I did catch a glimpse of her, I noticed the purple bruises and the black eyes. Even two doors away we could hear the cursing and swearing as Michael's dad showed what a big man he was. Occasionally, Michael would appear with bumps and bruises, but he would look at me in a way that made it clear it would be better not to ask how he got them.

I said Michael was a good reader; truth is, he was brilliant at everything. He was far and away the brightest in our class. I once overheard the headmistress say he was the cleverest child she had ever come across. So, when it came to transferring to secondary school, the headmistress wanted Michael to apply for a bursary to Hannah's old school. She told the Grants that she was certain Michael would breeze through the entrance exam. It could open the way to university.

All the fees would be paid for, but there would still be some costs involved. Mr Grant told the headmistress that they couldn't afford it. Anyway, Michael would be leaving school as soon as possible. He needed to be bringing money into the house.

So, Michael went to the same secondary school as I did. For the first two years, he was in the top group for every subject. Then one night we saw an ambulance at his door and his mother carried out on a stretcher. We never knew what happened for certain, but my mum reckoned that her husband hit her hard once too often.

Mrs Grant came home after a couple of weeks. I saw the police car outside Michael's house, but his dad was never charged with anything. I think Mrs Grant told them she had fallen down the stairs.

That's when I noticed the change in Michael. He just seemed to lose interest and his schoolwork suffered badly. I tried to ask him about it, but he just looked at me grim-faced and said there wasn't any point any more.

Then the ambulance came back to our street and Mrs Grant was carried out again – only, this time she didn't come back. We heard later that it was a blood clot on the brain.

My dad and I went to the funeral. I stood beside Michael,

who stayed as far from his father as possible. Mr Grant was obviously drunk, and blubbering like a baby. He was probably wondering who he could use as a punchbag, and who was going to buy his vodka for him now.

That night, I heard shouting and cursing coming from the Grant house. I rushed round, thinking that Mr Grant was taking out his grief on Michael. When I burst into the living room, I saw Mr Grant on the floor and Michael standing over him with a broken chair leg in his hands. His father's face was a bloodied mess.

'You killed her, you bastard!' Michael was yelling. 'All those years! I should have stopped you. Well, I'm stopping you now!'

I managed to grab Michael's arms before he killed his old man. Michael threw down the chair leg and walked out of the room. It was eight years before I saw him again.

Mr Grant moved out of the house soon after and, about a year later, there was a short piece in the paper. He had been found in an alley; he'd choked on his own vomit. I don't think anyone went to his funeral.

Over the years I received a few postcards from Michael, telling me that he was okay and not to worry about him. Some bore a Manchester postmark and one was from Spain, but there was never a return address.

Then one day I was at my desk when the doorman called to say there was someone in the hall to see me.

It was Michael. For the first time in our lives, we hugged. Then I stood back and took a good look at him. 'God, you look well,' I said. And he did. He was wearing a leather jacket that he didn't get in a charity shop, and he hadn't got his tan anywhere in Scotland.

I started to ask him the usual questions – when, where,

how, what – but he grinned and said, 'I can't stop right now. I've just come to invite you to dinner. Then I'll tell you all.'

Michael Grant inviting me to dinner – changed days from when we used to get a couple of bags of chips with my dad's money.

'Give me your address and I'll send a car for you,' he said. 'Say about seven?'

'No need,' I said. 'I'll meet you at the restaurant.'

He smiled. 'No, I'll send a car.'

That evening I was picked up in a chauffeur-driven Jaguar. We didn't stop in the centre of Dundee, but headed over the Tay Bridge. Twenty minutes later, we pulled up in front of the Old Course Hotel, in the home of golf – St Andrews. Michael was waiting to meet me.

I looked up at the magnificent building. 'You aren't actually staying here, are you?'

Michael smiled. He seemed to be smiling a lot these days. 'Just for a few days. Come on, let's eat.' Seconds later we were seated in the dining room.

I think we may have been the only two Scots in the room, and that included the waiters. Those actually speaking English were American and the rest were a mixture of Chinese, Japanese and Russian. They all had two things in common: they liked to play golf and they had very deep pockets. Given his complete lack of interest in sports, I was sure Michael hadn't come for the golf. So, what was he doing here and how could he afford it?

Over what was probably the best – and certainly the most expensive – meal of my life, Michael filled me in.

When he left his father bleeding on the floor, he found his dad's wallet and emptied it. He went to the bus station and asked how far he could get on the cash he had. He had been hoping to get to London. The answer was Manchester.

'Best thing that could have happened to me,' said Michael. 'I got off the bus and wandered around till I found a cafe looking for staff. They took me on, no questions asked, and I soon found out why. No one else wanted the job. For the next six months I did everything. I cleaned, waited tables and did some of the cooking. I even painted the bloody place once. The owner let me sleep in the back room and I got more in tips than I did in wages.

'There was this guy who came in every morning. Always the same order: tea and a fried egg on a roll. He used to bring in *The Times* to read, then leave it for me. The next day we'd discuss everything that'd been in the paper.

'One day, we were having an argument about politics when the cafe owner came over and told me there were other customers waiting. The guy just looked up at him and said Michael was busy. The cafe guy backed off right away, saying he was sorry for disturbing us.

'After six months, he said he had a job for me if I wanted it. I asked him why me? He said that he could see I was a hard worker and I had a brain. Those two didn't always go together.

'So, I joined the guy's organisation and gradually worked my way up.'

'Sounds amazing,' I said. 'But what kind of business are you in?'

Another smile. 'Boring stuff really. I kind of deal in commodities.'

My eyes tend to glaze over when I hear words like 'commodities', so I didn't press it, but I went on, 'So what are you doing back here?'

'I've been doing some research and I believe there may

be opportunities in this area. If it all goes well, I could end up running my own business here.'

I didn't have a clue about business, so I never questioned it. I was to find out what kind of 'commodities' Michael dealt in some time later. At the end of the meal, Michael walked me out to the car. He gripped my arm and said he would be heading back south but, if all went well, soon he would be back for good.

'That would be great,' I said. 'The old team back together. Remember all those battles we fought when we were kids?'

Michael looked serious. 'You were the first friend I ever had. I'll never forget what you did for me.'

As I sat in the back of the Jag on the way home, it occurred to me that Michael hadn't ordered any alcohol throughout the whole meal.

I didn't hear from Michael for another two months. Then I got a call at the office. Everything had gone to plan and he had moved up here. He was renting a flat till he found somewhere permanent. He wanted to celebrate.

'Not the Old Course again,' I said. 'Been there, done that.' We journalists can be a witty lot.

He laughed. 'No, somewhere even better. I'll meet you after work.'

'Shouldn't I go home and get changed first?'

'No, not necessary.'

After work, Michael was waiting for me on the steps. 'Follow me,' he said.

It was only a five-minute walk, taking us around St Mary's church tower, better known as the Old Steeple, which is Dundee's oldest surviving building. It dates back to the fifteenth century, although there has been a church on the site since 1190. The trouble was that the English, good Christians that they were, kept invading Dundee. For some reason, they took a dislike to the church, which they destroyed twice and damaged a third time. But Dundonians are a stubborn bunch. They kept rebuilding it.

A short distance beyond the tower we stopped, and Michael made an extravagant sweep of his arm. There in front of us was another Dundee icon, the Deep Sea Restaurant.

'Remember when your dad used to stand us bags of chips? My turn now. I might even be able to stretch to fish suppers!'

The Deep Sea was a Dundee institution. As you entered, there was a counter where you could order chips with just about anything to take away. No Mars bars though – that's a myth. Then, you passed through into a large room set with tables and chairs. The restaurant had opened in 1937, and rumour had it that some of the original waitresses were still serving. But they were so smart and efficient that they put their much younger counterparts in more esteemed dining establishments to shame. None of the customers were speaking Russian or Japanese, I noticed. There was a couple at a corner table speaking what appeared to be a foreign language, but my guess was that they were from Forfar.

We decided against the healthy eating option, which meant we didn't have peas with our deep-fried haddock and chips. With a side order of bread and butter, and washed down with strong cups of tea, it couldn't be beaten. Old Course, eat your heart out.

'I'm going to be really busy over the next few weeks,' Michael said. 'But, as soon as things are running smoothly, I'll get in touch again.'

However, months passed and I still didn't hear from him. He hadn't given me a phone number or an address, so I didn't know how to contact him.

When I did finally see him again, it was in the court in Dundee. I was covering the trial of a local man who had been stopped with a kilo of cocaine in the boot of his car. He pleaded guilty. I was taking notes, so I didn't notice Michael until he got up from the rear of the public gallery and left. I rushed out to catch him and almost ran into George.

'Hey! What's all the rush?' he said.

'Can't stop. I've just seen Michael Grant. You remember him?'

George put his hand on my arm. 'Ah, yes, Allan. I've been meaning to have a word with you about that.'

'I'll just be a minute,' I said, shrugging myself free. I ran out into the street. Michael was just getting into a car that had pulled up on the double yellow lines. I couldn't see the driver clearly.

'Michael! Where have you been?' I asked.

He glanced up to where George stood at the top of the steps, looking down at us. 'Sorry, Allan, I have to go. I'll be in touch soon, I promise.' He got in the car, which sped away. I could see Michael looking back at me.

George joined me. 'Come on, mate. Let's go to my office. We can talk there.'

His office was just a short walk from the court. A few minutes later we sat facing each other across his desk.

George was always good at getting straight to the point – not a trait he shared with every lawyer I've met.

'That guy you saw pleading guilty in court? He works for Michael.'

'So?' I said. 'Michael deals in commodities. If one of his

employees commits a crime, what's that got to do with him?'

George took a deep breath. 'Michael is a dealer all right, Allan, but the commodity he deals in is cocaine.'

At this point, I should have said that there must be some mistake, but I had known George almost as long as I had known Michael. George didn't say things like that without good reason.

'I know some of the guys in the procurator fiscal's office,' he went on. 'They're sure that in the last six months, Michael Grant has taken over as the major – no, the *sole* – distributor of cocaine in Dundee and the surrounding area.'

I still had a lingering doubt. 'Then why haven't they charged him? Why wasn't he in the dock today?'

'Because they need proof. Michael has been very careful and he's totally ruthless. He's never anywhere near the stuff. Between him and the guys on the street doing the actual selling there are several layers of management, if you like. He runs the whole operation like a major business. Which it is, I suppose.'

He sighed and continued, 'The cops have picked up a few guys like the one you saw in court today. They've been offered deals to testify against Michael. All have claimed to be acting on their own. One guy, without naming names, told the cops that if he kept his mouth shut, he knew that his family would be looked after. I bet that's what Michael was doing in court today – making sure his employee was doing what he was told.'

'I've been covering crime in Dundee for the paper for the last couple of years,' I said. 'I've never even heard a whisper about Michael being involved in drugs. Why do the cops think he is?'

'I understand that a few months back they got a tip-off

from their colleagues in Manchester. One of their inform-
ants had told them about a young Scots guy who'd been
working for a major drug dealer down there. This young
guy was coming back home to take over the cocaine trade.
The Manchester cops never got a name, or where the young
guy came from, but within a few weeks the drugs scene in
Dundee changed. Up till then, there had been a few different suppliers bringing coke into the city. The cops soon
noticed that a couple of them seemed to have left town in a
hurry, while another was found with two broken arms. The
story was that he was held over a toilet seat in a local pub
while the deed was done with a sledgehammer. Michael was
nowhere near it, of course. He has other people to carry out
the rough stuff.'

George paused, then said, 'I remembered you telling me
about Michael coming back here. Well, that's when all this
kicked off.'

Any doubts I had were seeping away. Michael had admitted that he'd been in Manchester for the last eight years.
His story about the guy in the cafe who offered him a job?
Maybe fried egg rolls were the breakfast of choice for drugs
barons in Manchester.

Then there was the question of Michael's new-found
wealth. Not many guys in my social circle stayed at the Old
Course and were chauffeured around in Jaguars.

I admit I hadn't inquired too closely about his new
'career', but when you turn your life around, wouldn't you
want to tell your best pal every detail? Then I remembered
what my dad had said all these years ago. Pals stick up for
each other. I had to speak to Michael; maybe, just maybe,
there was another explanation.

When I told George this, he leaned forward in his chair.

His expression was grim. 'My advice? Stay well clear of Michael Grant. The reason you haven't heard about this before is that the cops are keeping a tight lid on it. But when they finally get the proof they need, they'll be down on Michael like a ton of bricks. You don't want to get caught up in any of that. And another thing; don't be writing anything in the paper either. I don't want this coming back to me.'

I promised I wouldn't write a word, but I didn't promise that I wouldn't try to speak to Michael. Problem was, I still had no idea how to get in touch with him. However, that problem was solved a few days later, when a letter was delivered to my office, addressed to me. It simply said, 'THE OLD QUARRY. TONIGHT 7.'

Not far from the housing estate where Michael and I had grown up, there was an old quarry. There, you would find ancient rusting equipment and even an abandoned lorry. It was the kind of place that would send the health and safety fanatics apoplectic nowadays, but was once the ideal playground for a couple of daft laddies like us.

The track leading to the quarry was now overgrown and had been fenced off with barbed wire, but there were a couple of gaps big enough to squeeze through. Maybe not every kid in Scotland was sitting in front of a screen after all.

Michael stepped out from behind the old lorry. He smiled at me. 'Remember this place? Good times, eh?'

It would have been good to reminisce, but that childhood seemed a long time ago now. 'What's going on, Michael?' I said. 'Why are we meeting here like this?'

Michael's smile had gone. 'I saw you speaking to George and I've been wondering what he said to you. I thought it best if we spoke in private.'

'Well, guess what George told me?' I said. 'Apparently

you're Dundee's Mr Big in the drugs world. At first I couldn't believe it, but now I'm not so sure.'

As I spoke, Michael's face darkened, just as it had all those years ago. Then it cleared and he said, 'Okay, but first I have to ask you. Are you wearing a wire?'

I exploded. 'For fuck's sake, Michael! Who do you think you're talking to?'

'Sorry,' he said. 'I should've known better.'

Michael talked for the next twenty minutes. He basically confirmed everything that George had told me. There was probably a lot more he could have said, but I got the impression he wanted to keep the details to a minimum. I didn't feel angry. All I could think was, what a waste.

When he had finished, there was a silence for a few moments. Then I said, 'Michael, you were the cleverest guy I knew. You could've done anything. Why this?'

'Oh, yeah,' he said, and, for the first time, he sounded angry. 'I could still be working in that bloody cafe. I was fifteen. I was in a strange city, with no friends and no family. Then Kev –' Michael stopped before he gave the guy's name. 'Then someone gave me an opportunity. When I realised what he did, I thought, wait a minute, what am I getting myself into? Then I remembered my dad and his drinking. My life was made a misery because of alcohol, and Mum went through hell.' Michael smiled bitterly. 'The irony was that Mum never drank a drop in her life, and it ended up killing her. So, you have all these big alcohol corporations churning out this stuff that ruins lives. Their big bosses are paid fortunes – some of them become sirs! – but that's all right because everyone likes a drink. But if you do a line of coke now and again, that's bad. Explain that to me.'

I'd heard that argument before. 'It's not as simple as that –' I began, but Michael interrupted.

'Actually, it is,' he said. 'I'm not an idiot. I know that drug-taking can cause all sorts of problems, but so does booze. So, why is one worse than the other?'

Michael smiled again, and the bitterness had gone. 'You know, people think everyone who takes drugs is some kind of loser junkie, but most of my best customers are professional people – like lawyers, architects, even some journalists. What do they call it? "Recreational" drug-taking. I provide a service to these people. I supply good quality product at reasonable prices. What I don't do is sell crap like ecstasy, and other bad shit.'

I didn't think it would be a good idea at this point to mention sledgehammers or people suddenly leaving town.

'I had some stupid idea that you'd never find out, Allan,' he said. 'That we'd always be friends.'

'I can't lie,' I said. 'I hate what you do. But as far as I'm concerned, we're still friends.' But I knew that something had changed, and so did Michael.

We climbed back through the gap in the fence. There was a car waiting for him at the end of the track. As he got in, he paused and handed me a slip of paper. 'Just in case you need it some day,' he said.

As the car drove away, I looked at the paper. All that was written on it was a mobile phone number.

I never mentioned our meeting to anyone. We still bumped into each other occasionally – Dundee isn't a big place – but there were no more dinners at the Old Course or fish and chips at the Deep Sea. Honestly? I missed him.

7

The door opened and Michael came out. 'Good to see you, Allan. How's the private eye business? You aren't investigating me, I hope.' His smile was a bit forced.

I shook my head. I didn't ask how his business was doing because I didn't want to know. I had heard that he had moved into property developing, but my guess was that he hadn't abandoned his old trade. Anyway, that was kind of what I was banking on.

We went inside and sat across from one another on couches just slightly smaller than aircraft carriers.

'It is good to see you,' he said, 'but I'm guessing this isn't a social call.'

'It isn't,' I said. 'I've been asked to find this girl. The name I have for her is Tina Lamont but I'm pretty sure that isn't her real name, which makes me think there might be something dodgy about her. I do know that she comes from Dundee. She stayed in London for a while before coming back here. I was wondering if you could ask your ... er ... connections if they've heard anything.'

Michael chuckled. 'You mean my connections in the criminal underworld?' He saw the expression on my face. 'Don't be embarrassed, Allan. I'm not offended. D'you have a photo of Miss Lamont?'

I handed over a copy. He studied it. 'Pretty girl. I don't know her, but I'll ask around.'

We talked for a few more minutes, then he looked at his watch. 'Sorry, Allan, but I've a meeting this afternoon. I'm buying some land.'

As I drove back to Dundee, I couldn't help wondering what would have happened if Michael had been allowed to take up that bursary all those years ago. He might have become a lawyer or an architect; he might even have been one of those using recreational drugs. The irony.

For the next couple of days I sat in the office and looked online some more, but there wasn't a sign of Tina Lamont. I didn't expect to hear from Michael any time soon, but I was a bit surprised that Niddrie didn't make an appearance. He had obviously taken his mission to keep an eye on young Clayton seriously. I dreaded reading the headline in my old paper – 'Dundee Man Arrested for Stalking Schoolboy'.

I just sat at my desk. I couldn't think what to do next. Maybe Niddrie would have some ideas. Maybe Michael would call with some vital information. Maybe I should have lunch.

I hadn't eaten since breakfast, so I decided to pick up my home city's very own contribution to the world of fine dining – the Dundee pie. It's basically a pastry shell, but what goes in the filling has defied cookery experts for decades. Let's just say you would have more chance of working out the recipe for Coca Cola. One thing's for certain, though, after eating a Dundee pie, you don't want to do anything too physical, like getting out of your chair, for example.

I was still recovering when Niddrie walked in. 'How did it go with Michael Grant?' he asked.

'As well as could be expected,' I replied. 'What about you?'

Niddrie's cheek muscles rippled.

'Okay,' I said. 'What's going on?'

'I've been keeping an eye on young Clayton, like you asked. Found something interesting.'

'Well, what is it?' I asked, a little impatient.

He looked at his watch. 'Perfect timing. Follow me. I'll explain on the way.'

We left the office and I followed Niddrie to a large multi-storey car park in the centre of the town. As we passed Ailsa's school, I heard the bell ring, signalling the end of lessons for the day.

We went up to the fourth floor, which was almost deserted. Niddrie led me to a brand new Mini Cooper, top of the range. The initials 'SC' had been hand-lettered in gold script on the driver's door. We parked our backsides on the bonnet and waited.

About ten minutes later, Scott Clayton came out of the lift and walked towards us. He stopped a few yards short and his face twisted into some kind of weird expression. I'm guessing that he thought it made him look tough.

'I know you. You're Linton. Well, get your arse off my car. You and that ape with you.'

I resisted the urge to boot him in the arse. Instead I said pleasantly, 'I'd like you to stay away from my daughter. And I'd be grateful if you could also tell all your pals that you've been telling a pack of lies about her.'

Clayton made the kind of noise you usually hear in a pigsty. 'And what are you going to do if I don't?'

Niddrie took over. 'I've been watching you, young man. And I've seen you making some purchases. Little cellophane bags containing white powder.'

Clayton didn't look quite so tough now. 'So what?' he blustered. 'You can't prove anything.'

Again, a ripple of cheek muscles as Niddrie pulled a monkey wrench from the pocket of his parka and showed it to the boy.

'Oh, I'm not going to prove anything. You see, I bought one of those bags myself and I've hidden it in your car. Now, you could try to find it, but you'd have to take your little pride and joy to pieces, and I'm guessing you're no mechanic. And you wouldn't want to ask your garage, would you?'

Clayton was pale in the face. Niddrie calmly continued, 'So, you're going to do what Mr Linton asks, or I'll place an anonymous call to the local bobbies, telling them exactly where to look. I believe your school has a strict no drugs policy. I don't think mummy and daddy would be too pleased if you were expelled, not after buying you this nice car.'

I thought for a moment that young Clayton was going to be sick, but he recovered and mumbled, 'All right. I'll do it. Whatever you say.'

We stepped away from the car and he got in. We watched as he drove off down the ramp, tyres squealing.

I turned to Niddrie and looked at him in disbelief. 'You bought drugs? Where did you hide them?'

Niddrie had a face of stone. 'I'm not telling you.'

I said he could be bloody irritating. 'Why not?'

'Because if you were interrogated, you'd reveal everything. I, on the other hand, have been trained to resist even the most brutal torture.'

As we left the car park I had a thought: they must be a pretty tough bunch in the Pay Corps these days.

8

The weekend arrived, and Niddrie said he would make the rounds of pubs and clubs to speak to the bouncers. I said that I would devote my considerable intellect to the problem of finding the elusive Miss Lamont. Niddrie looked blankly at me and said he didn't realise we were in that much trouble. We agreed to talk again on Monday morning. On balance, I thought that the bouncers were becoming our last, and best, hope.

On Sunday morning I had a call from Ailsa, asking if I would like to meet for coffee. Unlike her mother, she quite liked frequenting the establishments of those American tax dodgers. They're cool and, of course, she wasn't paying.

It was a bright, crisp day – the kind you often get on the east coast – so Ailsa decided we would sit outside at a table on the pavement. That way she could see and be seen.

She looked terrific. Thankfully, she had inherited her mother's sense of style. Actually, she couldn't have inherited it from me anyway because, as she so often reminds me, I have none. Comfort over fashion, as far as I'm concerned.

She wore chunky boots, brightly patterned tights and a sheepskin-lined leather jacket that might have been worn by one of our boys during the Battle of Britain. I think she was also wearing a skirt, but it was so short you could hardly see it under the jacket. I had long ago learned not to comment on the length of my daughter's skirts. I couldn't take any more huffing and rolling of eyes.

As various teenage boys passed and gave her appreciative looks, I managed to resist the temptation to box their ears and send them on their way. I did glower at them ferociously, but that didn't have any effect. I don't think any of them noticed me; they were too busy looking at Ailsa. In turn, she glanced sideways at them before turning her head away.

'Er, remember me?' I said. 'Your old dad? *You* invited *me* for coffee, remember?'

Ailsa turned to me with her most dazzling smile. Hah! They just got sideways glances. I got the kind of smile used to advertise expensive toothpaste.

'Sorry, Dad.' She took a sip of coffee and went on, 'I was wondering if you'd managed to do anything about my problem.'

'Matter of fact, I have. I don't think you'll be bothered by that rugby-playing oaf any more. I had a nice chat with him and made him see the error of his ways.'

'No Spanish Inquisition then?' she grinned. 'I googled it.'

'That wasn't necessary, though I did get a little help from Niddrie.'

'I bet that scared the shit out of Scott,' said Ailsa. I was about to tell her to mind her language, but she continued, 'Uncle Niddrie's a scary dude. I like him.'

Ailsa had taken to calling Niddrie 'Uncle'. Somehow, I had never thought of Niddrie as 'Uncle', but Ailsa was genuinely fond of him, and I was sure he was secretly pleased, though he never said so to me.

Ailsa suddenly remembered something. She dug into the

oversized bag she had brought with her and pulled out a large brown envelope, the kind for carrying photographs. She placed it on the table.

'There was another reason I wanted to see you. We had our photos taken at school. I thought you might like a few.'

They were the standard portraits taken by school photographers. One large head-and-shoulders shot of Ailsa in her blazer, smiling at the camera, plus a couple of small copies. I studied them for a minute or two before putting them back in the envelope. For a moment I thought of another girl photographed in a school uniform, the one I had been paid to find.

I leaned over and kissed my daughter on the cheek. 'Thanks, honey.'

We chatted for a little while, until a black Mercedes Coupé pulled up across the street. Ailsa waved at the driver. It was Hannah.

'Mum said she would come and pick me up. She doesn't like me using the buses.' I thought, if only Hannah knew. I'd never told her about the day I'd first met Niddrie.

We stood and Ailsa took my arm. 'Come and say hello.'

She sensed my hesitation and tugged at my arm. 'It's okay, Dad. I'm not going to try and get you two back together. I know that would never work. Mum is talented, ambitious and hardworking. You, on the other hand, you're' – she hesitated – 'well, you're you.'

'Have you ever considered a career in the diplomatic service?' I asked.

Ailsa grinned. 'I'll think about it. Come on, you can at least say hello.'

I walked Ailsa to the car. Hannah rolled down the window and smiled up at me. 'You're looking well, Allan.'

Hannah didn't look good; she looked stunning, and she was driving the car to match. She always knew how to accessorise. I glanced around. The teenage boys had switched their attention from Ailsa to her mother. In fact, just about every male on the street was pretending not to look at her. I saw one old lad, who must have been in his seventies, almost walk into a lamppost. She'd had that effect on me once, but not any more. We were friends – more acquaintances, really – held together now by our mutual love for our daughter. As another of my dad's heroes, Buddy Holly, once sang, love is strange.

'Thanks,' I said. 'You're looking not too bad yourself.' See, I can do understated.

Ailsa hugged me and said, 'That was great, Dad. See you again soon.' She jumped into the passenger seat. Hannah managed another brief smile before rolling up her window. The Merc purred away.

The old lad had recovered from his near miss with the lamppost and, as he passed me, he gave me a knowing look. 'They break your heart, don't they?' He was only half right. One had broken my heart, but the other one lifted it every time I saw her.

That night, I sat in my flat and looked at Ailsa's school photo. An idea was starting to form in my head. I'd teach Niddrie to mock my intellect.

9

The next morning Niddrie was late coming into the office. 'Just popped into the library,' he said as he sat down.

For someone who visited the library so often, I never actually saw him with a book. I just had to investigate further. I could simply ask him, of course, but, as he said, he had been trained to resist the most brutal torture.

Instead, I asked him how it went with the bouncers. 'No luck,' he said. 'There was one guy who said she looked familiar, but he wasn't sure. You have any ideas?'

I smirked at him, 'Actually, I do. If we could find the school whose uniform Tina is wearing in the photo, maybe we could track her down that way. Now, I know that the uniform doesn't belong to any of the Dundee schools, but what if she didn't actually attend a school here? What if she moved to Dundee after she left school?'

Niddrie looked sceptical. 'So, what are you saying? We check every school uniform in Scotland?'

'We don't have to. I've found out that there's a place just outside Edinburgh that supplies uniforms to schools all over the country. I've spoken to a Miss Laverty there and she's agreed to meet me this afternoon. She thinks she may be able to help.'

'Want me to come?'

'And have you sitting in the car complaining about my choice of music? No, you're all right.'

Niddrie had never actually voiced an opinion about what I played; he just made a noise between a grunt and a sigh. I can take a hint.

The journey took just under ninety minutes and for most of that time I listened to Steely Dan. Now I know that I gave the impression that my dad thought music died after 1970, but he still made a few exceptions, and one of those was the Dan. The early stuff at least – before, in his words, 'They went all funny.'

Dad was a drummer, but he loved lead guitarists and Steely Dan had two of the finest in Jeff 'Skunk' Baxter and Denny Dias. When 'My Old School' came on, I turned up the volume as far as it would go. And, as usual, I sang along and did my lead guitar impression during the solos. I got some funny looks from cars as they passed, though one guy in a brand-new Range Rover gave me a thumbs up. We Dan fans stick together.

Some rock stars barely made it past their thirties. Others faded into obscurity, and some are still playing – a few in stadiums and others in pubs. But only one became a consultant in missile defence to the US government. And that was Jeff Baxter. That's what I call taking your career in a new direction.

I turned off the CD player when I turned into the small industrial estate where the school uniform supplier had its premises. A few minutes later I was sitting in Miss Laverty's office. It was hard to guess her age – anywhere between thirty and fifty. She had short blonde hair and wore glasses.

I had explained over the phone who I was and my reasons for coming to meet her. Now some people are cagey when

71

they talk to a private investigator. Not Miss Laverty. She was almost bouncing up and down in her seat with enthusiasm.

'This is so exciting!' she said. 'Nothing like this has ever happened to me before. Can you talk to me about the case? Is it something big ... not a murder?!'

I hated to disappoint her. 'No, I'm just trying to find someone.'

I needn't have worried. Her enthusiasm was undimmed. 'Never mind. I'll do my best to help.'

I had brought along Tina's photo, so I passed it over to Miss Laverty, who took her time studying it.

She looked up at me. 'Is this the person you're looking for?'

'Sorry, I can't say. It's confidential.'

Miss Laverty looked seriously at me and nodded once. 'Say no more. I understand completely. My lips are sealed.'

I was beginning to really like Miss Laverty.

She took a magnifying glass from a drawer in her desk and examined the photo again. 'The colour and style of the blazer and skirt are not uncommon, but the badge isn't familiar.'

She must have noticed the look of disappointment on my face, because she added, 'But that's not to say I can't find it. I can't remember every badge, but we have records going back decades. If we supplied that badge, then I'll identify it.'

'That's asking an awful lot, Miss Laverty,' I said.

She leaned forward and confided, 'Actually, it can get pretty boring working here. Playing a part in your investigation will make a very welcome change – even if it isn't a murder.'

She held up the photo.

'Can I hold on to this?'

'Sorry, as I said, it's confidential. I can't really leave it with you.'

'No problem.'

She raked around her desk till she found a pencil and a sheet of paper. Then, with the photo in front of her, she started drawing. A few minutes later she held up the paper. She had copied the badge exactly.

'This is all I need,' she said, handing the photo back to me.

We shook hands at the entrance to her building. 'I'll call you as soon as I find anything,' she said. 'Now I'd better get on. I've a mystery to solve!' She scuttled back inside.

I didn't get back to Dundee till after six. No point in going into the office, so I went straight home. After Hannah and I had split up, I'd bought another flat in the Ferry. Now, apart from a plethora of good pubs, the Ferry also has a wide selection of fast food joints. I make a point of not going to any of them. Well, that's not exactly true. There is a fish and chip shop that cooks the fish and fries the chips while you wait. It had been a long day, so I indulged myself.

I was sitting at my table with a piece of fried haddock halfway to my mouth when my mobile rang. The caller ID was blocked but I had a hunch who it was. I was right. It was Mr Carter.

'Ah, Linton,' he said. 'I'd like a progress report.'

I could have been completely honest and said there hadn't been much progress, but I thought about my conversation with Michael and Miss Laverty's enthusiastic response, so I was economical with the truth and said, 'I have a couple of leads which look promising, and my colleague and I will be following up on them.'

There was a pause on the other end of the phone. Mr Carter was probably having to take his time to digest all this information at once. Then he said, 'Very well. I'll call again in the next few days.'

He hung up.

10

The following morning, I went into the office. I sorted out my mail. It was mainly junk, but there was a letter from a lady who asked if I could find her missing cat. One for Niddrie, I thought. He seemed to have a thing about putting 'Missing' posters on lampposts.

Then, my phone rang. It doesn't sound like Abba's greatest hits or the '1812 Overture'. It actually rings, like phones used to do. Which makes it distinctive these days, I suppose. It was Michael Grant.

'I made a few calls over the weekend,' he said. 'Sorry, Allan, I can't help.'

'Thanks anyway, Michael.'

'Keep in touch. I'd like to know how this works out.'

I promised I would, but that was one of my 'promising leads' gone. I wasn't looking forward to Mr Carter's next call.

I've been asked how people can simply disappear. Believe me, it's a lot easier than you think. And Tina Lamont, or whoever she was, seemed to have been really good at it. Maybe she had lied to Carter's client. Maybe she told him she came from Dundee so that he would never find her. She could be anywhere in the world, which made the chances of

Allan Linton and Associates locating her as likely as a Tory winning a parliamentary seat in Dundee.

I had told Carter that I would do my best to find Tina Lamont, but I couldn't make any promises. Maybe it was time to admit that my best wasn't good enough. I decided to give it till Carter called again. Maybe Miss Laverty would have solved the mystery of the school uniform by then. Maybe Niddrie or I would bump into Tina Lamont in the street.

My thoughts were interrupted by a text from Niddrie. He had a few things to see to, so, unless there was anything urgent, he would see me tomorrow. I decided not to inflict the missing cat on him, so I texted back to say that would be okay.

Speaking of the cat, I read the letter again. It was beautifully handwritten, the kind of calligraphy you rarely see these days. Punctuation and grammar were immaculate. It was signed by a Miss D. Morrison, and I imagined an old spinster lady sitting at her writing desk, composing it with care. It was actually a pleasure to read it. The least it deserved was a reply. So I explained that we didn't have the requisite expertise to locate missing pets. However, if I could make a suggestion ... if she had a photo of her cat, she could have copies made and stick them on lampposts and bus shelters with a contact phone number.

That was the most productive thing I did for the rest of the day. I sat and stared at the wall for a while then turned on the small television I had in the corner of the room. I clicked through the channels. Most seemed to be showing cookery programmes. Niddrie hates them with a passion – 'Why would anyone want to waste their time watching other people making the dinner?'

I switched to the news for a while, but turned it off before I lost the will to live. The day a politician replies to a question by saying 'yes' or 'no' instead of 'before I answer that . . .' he or she will have my vote for ever.

I had printed off my letter to the cat lady, so I closed the office and headed out to post it before going home. On the way back to my car I passed the library and, for the first time that day, I had a flash of inspiration. No, not about finding Miss Lamont; maybe I could solve the mystery of Niddrie and what kept drawing him to the library.

I strolled into Dundee's Central Library and wandered through the different sections. No sign of my associate. I was on the verge of giving up, when I decided to check on the reading room upstairs. I was just about to enter through the glass doors when I saw Niddrie coming towards me. But he wasn't looking at me. As he passed the librarians' desk, he smiled at a woman on the other side. Niddrie smiling! Even more astonishingly, she smiled back. I looked closely at her. She looked about thirty, with light brown hair falling in gentle curls to her shoulders. Her smile was warm and genuine. 'Bye, Mr Niddrie. See you again soon.'

Niddrie spotted me. I was grinning all over my face. In contrast, his smile vanished without trace.

'Hello, Mr Niddrie.'

'What are you doing here?'

'Oh, just passing.' I inclined my head to the librarians' desk and raised my eyebrows. 'Pleasant lassie.'

Niddrie brushed past me. 'She'd just been helping me look something up.'

I knew better than to try to get anything more out of him. So, as we walked out, I filled him in on my meeting with Miss Laverty, and the calls from Carter and Michael.

'Not looking too good, is it?' he said.

'Unless Miss Laverty comes up with something, I think we're about done.'

Niddrie said he would walk me to my car. I had a parking space in a small square behind my office building. A narrow alleyway led from the street down to the square and, as most of the offices had closed for the day, it seemed deserted.

Not quite.

The back doors to some of the offices in my building were set into the walls of the alley. From the shadows of one of those doorways, three figures emerged. I recognised the one in the middle. It was Scott Clayton. Now Scott was a big boy, but his two sidekicks, though they were teenagers too, were even bigger and bulkier. They certainly towered over Niddrie and me. Scott grinned at me, but there was no humour in it. His two pals were doing their best to look hard and, to be fair, not making a bad job of it.

'Okay, Linton. I'm not taking any more of your shit.' He pointed at Niddrie. 'You tell me where you hid that stuff on my car or me and my friends will make you fucking suffer till you do.'

His grammar wasn't great – should have been 'my friends and I' – and I'm sure he didn't swear like that in front of his mum and dad. Then again, maybe he thought he had to sound hard as well as look it.

Niddrie shook his head. 'No, son, I'm not going to do that. Now why don't you all go home before someone gets hurt?'

Scott's face twisted and he took a step forward. 'Oh, someone's going to get hurt all right, you stupid bastard.'

I was wondering if Scott had used up his entire repertoire of naughty words when Niddrie took his right hand out of the pocket of his parka. Gripped in his fist was the monkey wrench. It looked bigger than I remembered. Maybe he had one for every occasion. Scott's pals seemed fascinated by its appearance.

'This is a monkey wrench, also known as an adjustable spanner. It's a versatile tool, but it can be used for all sorts of other things too.'

Scott tried to rally his troops. 'That's enough crap. They're just a couple of old guys. Get them!'

Old guys? No need for ageist insults.

Niddrie took his other hand out of his pocket and held it up. 'Hang on a minute, lads. Now, you're big strong lads, and Linton and I are – as Scott says – just a couple of old guys. The chances are you'll give us a right kicking. But I reckon we could do a bit of damage too before we're done here.'

Scott was going red in the face, but the other two were starting to look wary. Then Niddrie played his ace.

'Paul and Kenneth, isn't it? Thought I recognised you. You've both been picked for the final trials for the Scottish schools rugby team on Saturday, am I right? Congratulations.'

The two big lads actually took a step back.

Niddrie slapped the wrench into the palm of his left hand. 'But what if you got injured before the weekend? Broken hand maybe – or worse, your knee got messed up.'

'Don't listen to him, guys,' Scott pleaded. 'There's only two of them. We can take them.'

Paul looked at Kenneth – or was it the other way round? 'It's not worth it,' he muttered. 'Come on, Kenny.' Ah, I was right first time.

Niddrie and I stood aside as the lads moved past us and

walked down the alley. Scott screamed after them, 'Wait! Where're you going? You said you'd do this.'

Kenny didn't stop, but he looked back over his shoulder. 'You said it was going to be easy. You didn't say one of them was a nutter. Anyway, it's your own fault. I told you to stop using that stuff.'

Niddrie waved at the international hopefuls as they exited the alley.

'All the best for Saturday, lads. I'll be rooting for you.'

Scott looked like a spoiled brat who had just been stopped from kicking a puppy. I thought for a moment he was going to stamp his foot.

'It's over,' I said. 'I think it would be best if you followed your mates.'

As Scott took my advice, Niddrie said, 'That was a narrow escape.'

For just a second, my mind flashed back thirty years, to when I had stood at Michael Grant's side. I could remember the kicks and punches.

'You're telling me,' I replied. 'We could've been on the wrong end of a right doing.'

Niddrie snorted. 'No, I meant a narrow escape for them. They're big lads all right, but I seriously doubt if any of them have been in a real fight in their lives. Have you ever seen a so-called punch-up on a rugby field? All those big guys holding on to one another and flapping their hands till the referee steps in.'

Niddrie gestured around the alley. 'But this isn't a rugby field and there isn't a referee. It's a back alley. Here, you kick, stamp and gouge.' He looked at me as he slipped the wrench back in his pocket. 'And you use anything else you have to hand.'

I wondered if Kenny and Paul would ever realise how lucky they had been.

Niddrie's cheek muscles rippled. 'And, of course, I suppose you could have been some help if I'd really needed it.'

'Oh, thanks. But how'd you know about those two playing in the trials on Saturday?'

'I was in the reading room at the library, remember? Their picture was in the local paper.'

We reached my car. Trying hard to look innocent, I said, 'Oh, that's right. Where that nice young lady helped you look up something.'

There was just the hint of an intake of breath from Niddrie, so I said, 'See you in the office tomorrow?'

Niddrie nodded and I got into the Hyundai and drove home.

11

On the way to the office the following morning I bought a pair of picture frames. I was at my desk fitting Ailsa's school photos into them when Niddrie appeared. I offered one of the photos to Niddrie.

'I just got them from Ailsa. Thought you'd like one.'

Niddrie looked pleased. 'You won a watch with that one. But it's a good job she's got her mother's looks – and her brains.'

I placed the other frame on my desk.

'She's fond of her Uncle Niddrie. She thinks you're a scary dude.'

'I'll take that as a compliment.'

'From Ailsa it is.'

'You won't be mentioning last night's little tête-à-tête to her, will you?'

'No, I don't want to bother her with that. And I think we can be pretty sure that Scotty and his little gang won't be telling anyone either. I can't see them wanting anyone to know that they backed down to a couple of old guys.'

I grinned, 'Even if they thought one of them was a nutter.'

Niddrie frowned. 'Not sure if that was meant as a compliment. Anyway, what makes you think they were referring to me?'

Before I could reply, my phone rang. It was Miss Laverty. I put her on speakerphone.

'I'm so sorry, Mr Linton. I haven't been able to identify that school badge. I even spoke with a colleague in Glasgow. We're absolutely certain that no school in Scotland has a badge with that design on its blazers.'

'Don't worry, Miss Laverty. I really appreciate all your efforts. Thank you.'

'Of course, the girl in the photograph could be wearing the uniform of a school outside Scotland. England, Wales or even abroad. But I can't help you there, I'm afraid.'

'I understand. You did everything you could. I couldn't have asked for more.'

'Oh, I so wanted to help you solve the mystery.' She paused before going on, 'Can I ask a favour, Mr Linton?'

'Anything,' I said.

'If you ever solve the mystery of the missing girl, will you let me know?'

I promised I would and we hung up.

Niddrie looked at me, eyebrows raised.

'But we aren't going to find her, are we?' he said. 'We can't check every school in the world.'

I leaned back in my chair. I couldn't disagree. Then Ailsa's school photo caught my eye and I sat up.

'What if we've been looking at this the wrong way round?'

'What d'you mean?'

'Up till now we've just taken it for granted that Tina was wearing her own school uniform. But what if she wasn't? She could've been wearing that uniform in the photo for any number of reasons, like fancy dress, for instance. Carter said his client told him that Tina originally came from

Dundee. Let's assume she did and let's further assume that she did go to school here.'

I held up Ailsa's photo, and continued, 'If that was the case, she'd almost certainly have had her photograph taken at school, just like this.' I held up Tina's photo in my other hand. 'We could show this to photographers who specialise in school photographs. It must've been taken in the last few years. Maybe one of them would recognise the girl in it.'

For a second Niddrie looked impressed. 'Maybe I was wrong when I said that Ailsa got all her brains from her mother. But it's a pretty long shot. These guys must take hundreds of photos every year. And, think about it, you go and ask a photographer to help you find a schoolgirl and he might ask you to take a seat while he calls the police.'

'You're right, but there's one guy who may be able to help. It's worth a try and, let's face it, it's all we've got at the moment.' I stood up. 'I'll go and see him.'

'D'you want me to walk you to your car?' asked Niddrie. 'Just in case there are packs of unruly schoolboys lying in wait for you.'

'No, I think I'm safe. They should all be in class just now.'

We were just like two Olympic swordsmen, but duelling with words instead of rapiers, eh?

I drove out on the Perth Road to the West End of the city. This was where my great-grandparents had lived in an overcrowded tenement, more than a century ago. One of their five children – my granddad – once told me they had all lived in two rooms, with the toilet conveniently situated on the outside landing. They did have to share it with three other families but, on the upside, the jute mill where they laboured was less than a hundred yards away, so they had a short commute.

The mills and the tenements are all long gone now. The grim, grey stone buildings have been replaced by the sleek glass and concrete structures of Dundee University. Students come from all over the world to study here. The 'uni' has won all sorts of awards in recent years and has become renowned for its medical research. My granddad also told me that three of his siblings died before their tenth birthdays because their parents couldn't afford to pay for medical treatment.

The irony is that the co-founder of the university was the spinster daughter of one of the jute barons. She donated a sum that would be the equivalent of hundreds of millions of pounds today. Pity her dad and others hadn't paid their workers better. My great granddad might have been able to afford a doctor.

I managed to find a parking space just past a pub called the Speedwell Tavern, although no one calls it by that name. I remember once asking a local where it was and he looked blank for a few moments, before he said, 'Oh, you mean Mennie's!' Apparently, Mrs Mennie was the name of the landlady who ran the place for fifty years. I'm always wary of a pub with an identity crisis, so I just had the one pint and left.

I got out of the car and walked a few yards to the premises of Bruce McAllister, Photographer. It had been a shop at one time, but now the window was full of framed photos placed carefully on shelves lined with black velvet. Some were studio portraits of families and individuals, but there were a couple of black and white cityscapes and one of the River Tay at dusk. The river looked like molten lava in the setting sun.

Now, when it comes to art, I make the Philistines look like members of the Royal Academy, but even I could tell those latter photographs were stunning.

A little bell tinkled as I walked in the door and, seconds later, a heavy curtain at the back of the shop parted and a man in his early fifties emerged. He was of medium height and medium build. His brown hair, flecked with grey now, was cut short with a side parting. Bruce McAllister was the most unremarkable man I had ever met, except when it came to taking photographs. Then he was a genius. He stopped when he saw me, and a slow smile spread across his face.

'Allan ... Allan Linton. It's so good to see you.' He tilted his head to the side. 'But I'm guessing this isn't purely a social call.'

'Good to see you too, Bruce.' I hesitated before going on, 'But you're right. I'm working on something and I'm hoping that you may be able to help.'

'I think it would be best if we discussed this in private, Allan.'

Without another word, he walked over to the door and flipped the sign hanging there to read 'CLOSED'. Then he turned and led the way through the curtain to his studio.

Like the man himself, the room was immaculate. Bruce sat at an uncluttered desk and I took the seat facing him. I showed the photo of Tina Lamont to Bruce.

'I've been hired to find this girl. The only information I have is that she came from Dundee originally and, even though she is blonde in the photo, she's actually a brunette.'

He took it from me and studied it. Then he shook his head.

'This isn't a posed shot. Looks to me that it was taken with a phone or something similar. I've worked with all the local schools and I don't recognise the uniform. So how can I help?'

'I've established that no school in Scotland wears that uniform,' I said. 'But I'm hoping that the girl did go to school here and, if she did, she had her photo taken.'

Bruce smiled. 'Ah, I see. And you're hoping that, if your theory is correct, I took her photo and will remember her. That's a lot of hoping, Allan.'

'You're right,' I agreed. 'It was a long shot.' I reached out for the photo. 'I don't even know when it was taken,' I said. 'The girl could be in her twenties now. It's too much to ask.'

But Bruce held on to the photo.

'Perhaps not. Sometimes long shots pay off. Everything's digital these days and I keep all my school portraits going back years. Let me check and see if I can find her.'

'Are you sure, Bruce? It could be an awful lot of work for nothing.'

Bruce looked at me seriously. 'I once promised you that, after what you did for me, I'd do anything for you if I could. D'you remember? I meant every word, Allan.'

'If you do manage to trace her, you can trust me that I'll do nothing that could harm her. I won't tell the person who's looking for her where she is without her permission.'

Bruce laid the photo on his desk.

'Oh, I told you once before, I trust you, Allan. There's no one I trust more.'

12

I had earned Bruce's trust nearly three years before. I'd just been paid for exposing the scam at the pub and I was sitting at my desk, grinning at the bank statement I had just received. Normally, I opened the envelope just enough to take a quick peek at the bottom line, before closing it quickly and sticking it in my desk drawer. You know, a bit like the guy who holds up that stupid red box every year and lies about the state of the economy, only I bet he doesn't have to pay the overdraft charges.

Financially secure for the next month at least, I sat back in my chair and laced my fingers behind my head. There was a tentative knock on the door. Usually, I didn't bother to say 'Enter!' because people tended to come straight in after knocking. And at least one unhappy client had just burst in without bothering to knock.

But no one entered and, after a short pause, there were two more knocks, just as tentative as the first. I thought this could go on all day, so I called out, 'Come in.'

The door opened and a man took one step into the office.

'I'm looking for Mr Linton,' he said.

'You've found him,' I said. 'What can I do for you, Mr . . . ?'

'I'd prefer not to give my name for the moment.'

'I always like to know who I'm working for,' I said. I gestured to the visitor's seat. 'But in the meantime, why don't you sit down and tell me why you are here. Then I can tell you if I can help you and you can tell me your name.'

'Someone's trying to extort money from me,' he said.

I had once covered a case of extortion when I was a crime reporter. The extortionist had found out that his victim, a prominent local politician, was having an affair with a married woman who happened to be a member of another party. It hadn't ended well for anyone. The guy being extorted handed over some cash, but when the extortionist came back for more, the politician apparently said something along the lines of, 'Fuck that. She wasn't worth what I paid you the first time!' and proceeded to give his tormentor a kicking. The politician got eighteen months for assault and the extortionist received a year for demanding money with menaces. One thing I did learn from my time as a crime reporter: there's the law and then there's justice, and only rarely do the two meet.

So, I said to the man before me, 'Look, I'm not here to judge you. Anything you say within these four walls stays here. So, as long as it doesn't involve anything illegal, can you tell me why someone thinks you'll pay them to keep their mouths shut?'

The man slumped in the chair. 'I haven't done anything wrong. Someone's set me up.'

'Then why don't you go to the police?' I said.

The man looked panicked. 'Oh, I can't do that! Everything would come out.'

We were starting to go round in circles, so I said firmly, 'Start at the beginning and tell me everything. Then, if I can help you, I can assure you I will.'

The man sighed and said, 'You're right. It's just that I've been under a lot of strain recently. My name's Bruce McAllister and I'm a photographer. I do a lot of work in schools. You know, portraits of the children and their classes.'

I nodded, and he continued, 'Two weeks ago, I was working at one of the local secondary schools. There's always a teacher present when I take photos of individual pupils. I was about to take a photo of one girl – her name was Shania McKay – when the teacher was called away. Before she left, she asked if I wanted to take a break till she came back.

'We were already running late, mainly due to the unruly behaviour of the pupils and, quite frankly, I just wanted to get the whole thing over with. So I said I'd carry on. The teacher said she'd be as quick as she could and left. Another girl came into the room and I told her to wait.' Bruce shook his head. 'How could I have been so stupid? The teacher was gone for about ten minutes. In that time I managed to get the girl to stop behaving badly so I could take her picture.

'Anyway, I didn't give it another thought till last week, when the McKay girl and her mother appeared in my shop. They accused me of – how did the mother put it? – "interfering" with her little girl. She said that if I didn't pay her £5000, she would go to the press. I should say at this point that her "little girl" is sixteen and bigger than I am.'

Bruce sighed, his face flushed with anger. 'I told her to get out. I hadn't done anything to her awful daughter. She was making it all up! But then that horrible woman said she had a witness ... the other girl – the one I'd asked to wait. Apparently, she was willing to swear that she'd seen me touching her friend and making disgusting suggestions.

'The mother said I had a week to get the money or she'd

go to the papers. They'd pay for her story. She even said she could see the headline – "School Photographer in Child Abuse Scandal".'

Bruce looked close to tears, but I had to ask the question. 'You did absolutely nothing that could have been taken the wrong way? Did you touch the girl, even totally innocently?'

Bruce sat upright. I've never seen anyone look so indignant. For a moment I thought he was going to run out of my office.

'No, I did nothing! I have no interest in girls.' He slumped forward, dropping his head into his hands. 'Don't you see? I'm gay!'

I knew that I had to tread very carefully at this point, so I took a deep breath and said, 'It would be very helpful if ... how can I put it ... if you could provide proof of your sexual preferences.'

Bruce looked distraught. 'I can't ... I won't. I will not have my private life put in the public domain. I look after my mother, who is now in her eighties. She knows nothing about ... about this side of my life. She's very old-fashioned in her views and I'll not subject her to any kind of distress.'

Bruce paused and frowned at me.

'I'm gay, but I am not a paedophile. I've no interest in young boys, just as I'm not attracted to girls of any age. But even in this so-called "enlightened age", there are those who'd call for me to be banned from working in schools. And I've little confidence that the schools would stand up to those who are so easily offended.'

Bruce looked at me pleadingly. 'I need someone to prove that the girls are lying and that the mother is doing this just to get money out of me. But I'll not reveal that I'm gay!'

91

I had no doubt that Bruce McAllister was a decent man and he didn't deserve to be tormented by those scheming creatures.

'I believe you,' I said. 'After all, what kind of a mother would try to make money out of her daughter being assaulted?' I snorted. 'My guess is that the daughter told her mum about being left alone with you and the pair of chancers eventually worked out it could be a quick and easy way to make some cash. If you had paid her, that wouldn't have been the end of it, either. She'd have milked you dry.'

I thought for a moment, then said, 'I think I may be able to help you, Mr McAllister.'

For the first time, I saw some hope in Bruce's eyes.

'Please, call me Bruce. Of course, I'll pay you, whatever it costs.'

'I think you'll find my fee is a lot less than £5000 and I can start right away. What information can you give me about the McKays?'

Bruce reached into his pocket and pulled out a small photo of a teenage girl. She wasn't wearing a blazer, but I recognised the school tie knotted loosely round her neck in a fashion that she probably thought made her look cool. I thought she just looked scruffy. She was wearing make-up, but it looked as if it had been applied by a bricklayer who hadn't had his eyes tested for a while.

'This is Shania,' he said. 'I don't have an address, but the mother gave me this.'

He handed me a slip of paper with a mobile number scrawled on it. 'I am to phone her when I have the money.'

'That's enough to get me started. D'you have a card – so that I can contact you if I need to?'

Bruce gave me the numbers of his shop phone and mobile.

I said, 'I need as much time as I can get. So, if they phone you asking for the money, put them off. Say you're having to sell your car to raise the cash. You'll think of something.'

I got up and saw Bruce to the door. The relief was evident on his face as he turned to face me.

'Thank you so much, Mr Linton. I was at my wits' end. I just didn't know who to turn to. I'm so glad that I took a chance and came to you.'

'Call me Allan,' I said. 'And don't worry. I don't think we're dealing with criminal masterminds here.'

For the first time since he came into my office, Bruce smiled at me.

'I'm not worried now, Allan. I trust you.'

After Bruce left, I looked at the photo of the lovely Shania again, then checked my watch. If I moved now, I could catch her as she left school.

Half an hour later I was driving into a housing estate called Kirkton. The tie I had recognised in Shania's photo was the only form of school uniform worn by the pupils at the local secondary school. I had lived in a similar estate while growing up and I knew that the people who lived in places like that were a mixture of good and bad. But I remembered a conversation I had once had with the pharmacist at the local chemist's shop. He had told me that they dispensed methadone in almost industrial quantities.

I parked on the other side of the road, about fifty yards from the school. Five minutes later, the doors opened and the kids were disgorged. It wasn't hard to spot Shania; she was the biggest kid in the crowd, in both height and breadth. By contrast, the girl walking beside her was short and stick thin. They were talking on their mobile phones, probably to each other. I guessed that this was the witness.

A boy of about twelve bumped into Shania as he ran past. It wasn't his fault; she was taking up most of the pavement. Shania interrupted her phone conversation to scream a torrent of foul-mouthed abuse at him.

I got out of the car and followed them. Eddie McLaren had taught me various techniques for tailing someone without them knowing it. I didn't need them here. Shania and her little pal were so engrossed in their phones that I could have been behind them in a tank and they wouldn't have noticed.

The girls stopped at the gate of a semi-detached house. If you had wanted to preserve any wildlife, there was no better spot to hide the creatures than the front garden. No one would have ever found them in there.

The girls exchanged hugs and, to my amazement, air kisses. The pal had to stand on her toes and even then she barely made it to Shania's chin. The pal walked off and Shania went into the house. I parked across the street and settled down to wait.

An hour later, a woman walked up to the house, carrying a large container from a fast food outlet. There was no mistaking the family resemblance.

I had already decided to concentrate on the mother, but I didn't have to follow her any distance, because she never went very far. She never left the house before midday, and even then she would just walk to the nearest shops to stock up on cigarettes and stodge. Pies, pizza and burgers, washed down with fizzy drinks, seemed to be the ambrosia and nectar of the McKay family. There was no sign of any male occupant in the house.

One afternoon, she went into a small corner shop and didn't come out for a couple of hours. I looked inside and saw her behind the counter serving a customer.

The weekend was approaching and I had a hunch about how Kirkton's candidate for 'Mother of the Year' would spend it. I was outside her house on Friday evening when Shania's friend arrived. A few minutes later she and Shania left the house. They hadn't even reached the front gate before they started speaking into their phones.

Then, about an hour later, the mother came out. She had made an effort and dressed up. The leggings and hoodie had been left in her wardrobe and she was wearing a skirt and a short jacket over a blouse. She tottered down the street in high heels and I followed. My hunch proved correct: she went into the local bar. I waited a few minutes then went in after her.

When the big estates were being built on the outskirts of Dundee, the planners made provision for all the necessary amenities. So, they all had a couple of rows of shops, a church and at least one big pub. At first, a lot of these places had been privately owned. I can remember my gran and granddad getting dressed up on a Saturday night to spend the evening in the Dolphin Bar in Fintry. They always went to the upstairs lounge, where the owner would only serve beer in half-pint glasses. Seriously. The only other place I'd heard of that had this policy was the bar in the Ritz Hotel in London. My granddad got round this by ordering two half pints at a time. In the Dolphin, I mean, not the Ritz.

But, over the years, the estate pubs had been taken over by the big brewers. In my experience, that is the kiss of death for a bar. Most of them were now just drinking dens. If the bar staff had insisted on serving only half pints they would have been lynched.

I stood for a few minutes in the pub doorway, letting my eyes adjust to the gloom. There was a long bar to my right and booths lining the wall on the left. Shania's mum had just been served and was picking up a glass when I moved towards her.

I bumped against her elbow as she turned from the bar. Most of her drink spilled onto the carpet. She looked down at it for a moment, then back up at me.

'You stupid prick!' she snarled at me. 'I'd just bought that drink.'

I held up a hand. 'Sorry, darling,' I said. 'It's a bit dark in here. Let me buy you another. What was it?'

She sniffed. 'Vodka and coke. A double.'

I nodded to one of the empty booths. 'Why don't you take a seat and I'll bring it over?'

I turned to the barman and ordered her drink. When I specified a double, he raised his eyebrows and shook his head, but I just grinned at him.

'It's okay,' I said. 'I know. And I'll have the same, but without the vodka.'

As I picked up the drinks, he muttered, 'Good luck, mate.'

The carpet was sticky underfoot as I walked over to the booth. Obviously, drinks being spilled in this pub was not a rare occurrence.

I placed her drink on the table. She didn't bother thanking me; she just took a large swallow and sat back. At first I thought she had a pimple on her nose, then I realised it was a gold stud. At least she wasn't a walking ironmongers.

'Look, I'm sorry about that,' I said. 'I'll leave you in peace now.'

She tilted her head back and looked up at me. Then she patted the seat beside her. 'What's your hurry?'

I sat down next to her and she smiled. It wasn't the most pleasant experience of my life, but I grinned back at her. Eddie had once told me that a good investigator should be a good actor. After this, I thought I might audition for RADA.

'I haven't seen you in here before,' she said.

'No, I'm visiting a mate who lives near here. We're doing a bit of business. He had to go out for a while and I didn't fancy being stuck in the house.'

'I know what you mean. Er, what kind of business are you in?'

I took a sip of my drink. 'Let's just say my friend obtains stuff and I help find buyers for it.'

She held up a hand. 'Say no more. I didn't mean to pry.' She quickly swallowed the rest of her drink.

'Another?' I said.

'Oh, if you insist.' She held out her hand. 'I'm Nikki, by the way.'

I shook her hand. It was surprisingly soft. Well, I guessed she didn't wash many dishes.

'Chaz. Nice to meet you.'

I went back to the bar and ordered another double. As he placed the drink on the bar, the barman said, 'You don't have to keep buying her doubles, you know. After this one you can make it singles. She won't know the difference.' He winked.

For the next two hours, I pretended to be interested in Nikki's hard-luck life story. She'd had her little precious, Shania, when she was sixteen, which made her just thirty-two. I had thought she was in her forties. The girl's father had done a runner before Shania was born and she didn't know where he was, so she had had to struggle on her own. Her parents had wanted her to stay at home with the child, but she was determined to be independent. Fair enough, I thought. Until, in an indignant outburst, she demanded to know how she was expected to live on the benefits she received. Like I said, she was determined to be independent.

She'd even had to take a part-time job in one of the local shops. Just a few hours a week, cash in hand, so that she could afford a few of life's little luxuries – like Shania's state-of-the-art phone, I supposed.

As the night wore on, I took the barman's advice and just bought singles for her. He was right. It didn't make any difference. She was becoming pissed just as quickly, but for half the price. I stuck to the Coke, but I pretended I was becoming a bit tipsy too.

Every time I came back from the bar I noticed that one of the buttons on her blouse had become undone. I had just bought another round when she leaned forward and revealed a cleavage deep enough to accommodate a small car. She put her hand on my thigh and smiled groggily at me.

'But my luck is about to change,' she slurred. 'I'm coming into some money very soon. Thousands.'

'That's great,' I said, but I didn't press her. I knew I didn't have to. She was just dying to tell someone.

'I can trust you to keep a secret, can't I?' she said in a conspirator's whisper.

I nodded my head, my eyes half closed. I can do conspiratorial when I want to. 'Sure you can.'

An audition for RADA? Just nominate me for a BAFTA now.

'There's this wee shite. He took Shania's school photo.

I've told him he has to pay me five grand or I go to the papers saying he interfered with her.'

I sat up, looking confused. 'How's that going to work? It'd just be her word against his.'

Nikki smirked. 'Thought of that. Shania's wee pal Kylie is going to say she saw the whole thing. I'll slip her a few quid, of course.'

'That's brilliant,' I said.

Nikki sat up, swaying, but looking very pleased with herself.

'Fucking right it is. And that's not all. I'll just keep going back for more money. He'll have to pay up or he'll be finished. It's ... What do you call it? The gift that just keeps on giving.'

She slumped back in her seat, exhausted by the explanation of her master plan.

I pulled my phone from my pocket and looked at it. It hadn't made a sound, but in her present state there was no way that Nikki would have realised.

'Text from my mate,' I said. 'He's come back. Sorry, darling, I have to go.'

Nikki looked at me with bleary eyes. 'Oh, I thought we could go on somewhere.'

I thought that if she got as far as her front door she would be doing well.

Nikki pursed her lips and leaned forward. I'm not that good an actor. I smiled and got up.

'It's been great,' I said.

'See you again?' she asked hopefully.

I stopped and looked back with a wink. 'Oh, you can bet on it.'

She smiled and waggled her fingers at me.

As I passed the barman, he smirked. 'Leaving us so soon?'

'She's all yours,' I said.

The barman looked grim. 'No thanks. Been there, done that.' Then he shuddered and added, 'Not doing it again.'

Next morning I phoned Bruce.

'I want you to call the McKay woman and tell her you want to see her at your shop. I'd leave it till a bit later in the day. She's not what you'd call a morning person – this morning in particular. Call me when you've set up the meeting.'

Bruce said he would organise it and rang off.

It was almost 5 p.m. before the bell above the door of Bruce's shop tinkled and Nikki and Shania entered. Bruce came out from his studio to greet them.

Even the several millimetres of make-up plastered on her face couldn't hide the fact that Nikki was as white as a sheet.

'I'm not feeling all that good,' she mumbled. 'I thought I was going to be sick in the taxi. The cabbie was gonna throw me out till I told him he'd get a bang in the jaw.'

She paused to swallow.

'Never mind that. Got my money?'

'No,' said Bruce.

Nikki's eyes narrowed.

'I warned you. The money, now, or I'll fucking ruin you.'

Bruce looked her right in the eye. 'I'm not giving you any money, now or ever.'

Bruce flinched as Nikki screamed and lunged at him.

'You bastard!' she cried.

That's when I stepped out from behind the curtain. Just in time, as Nikki's hands were inches from Bruce's throat.

Nikki pulled up short. Her jaw actually dropped. I think it's fair to say she was astonished.

Shania glared at me. 'Who the fuck are you?' she asked.

'Chaz?' said Nikki. She had moved on from astonished to totally baffled. 'What are you doing here?'

'My name isn't Chaz. I'm a private investigator working for Mr McAllister.'

Nikki's jaw worked, and she drew back her head.

I said, 'If you spit on me, I'll break your nose.'

'You lying shite. You got me drunk.'

'Not the most difficult job I've ever had, I have to admit.'

I took a small object about the size of a cigarette lighter from my pocket and held it up.

'This is a recording device,' I said. 'I had it in my pocket last night. Let's listen, shall we?'

We got as far as the part where Nikki said that Bruce would have to pay up or he'd be finished, before she said, 'Okay, that's enough.'

'Right,' I said. 'Here's what's going to happen. You'll leave now and you'll never have any contact with Mr McAllister ever again. If you don't do as you're told I'll take this recording to the police.'

It was Shania's turn to be baffled. 'Does that mean we're not gonna get any money, Mum? I thought we were going to Florida.'

Nikki grabbed her daughter's arm and pulled her out of the shop. 'This is all your fault, you stupid cow, telling me about getting your photo taken.'

I have to say, I thought that was a bit unfair.

When Nikki and her little precious had gone, I locked the door and put up the 'CLOSED' sign. I turned to Bruce. He was actually shaking.

'That was amazing,' he gushed. 'It was like something out of a James Bond movie.'

I held up my little device. 'Oh, you mean this thing? My old boss bought it on the internet; it's been lying in a drawer ever since. This is the first time I've had the chance to use it. Worked a treat, eh?'

Bruce took a deep breath and stopped quivering. I smiled at him.

'It's over,' I said. 'I'll send you my bill next week.' I smiled. 'I tried to keep my expenses to a minimum, but I had to pour a fair amount of vodka down Nikki's throat, I'm afraid.'

'Worth every penny,' said Bruce.

He clasped my right hand in both of his.

'I can't thank you enough, Allan.'

And that was when he promised to do anything for me if ever he could.

13

A couple of days after I asked Bruce for his help in search-
ing for the mysterious Tina, Niddrie and I were sitting in
my office. I had told him about my visit to Bruce's studio,
but he was sceptical.

'First of all, you're hoping that this Bruce guy took the
girl's photo, then you're hoping that he can find her in his
files. I'll say this for you, Allan. You're ever the optimist.'

I looked up at the ceiling and remembered a line from a
dire movie I'd watched one afternoon when I was sprawled
on the couch wrapped in my duvet and full of a cold.

'When all you've got is hope, you have to go on hoping.'

'In other words, if this guy, Bruce, doesn't come up
trumps, we're fucked,' said Niddrie.

'That's another way of looking at it,' I admitted.

That was when my phone rang. It was Bruce.

'I think I may have found something,' he said. 'Come
and take a look.'

I hung up and looked at Niddrie.

'We're not fucked yet. I'm going to see Bruce. Want to
come? I promise not to play anything in the car.'

Bruce was waiting for us. I could see a slight look of
apprehension when he saw Niddrie enter the shop with
me. I gave him a slight shake of the head and he seemed

reassured. I had once promised Bruce that I would never tell anyone about his sexuality, and I had kept that promise. I hadn't even told Niddrie.

I introduced Niddrie, and Bruce led us into the studio. A laptop was sitting on his desk. He pressed a key, and a head-and-shoulders shot of a teenage girl popped up on the screen. She was wearing the blazer of a school situated in the West End of Dundee. She had mid-length brown hair and she was looking solemnly at the camera. Niddrie and I looked at each other.

'It's her,' he said.

The hair was a different colour – Carter had been right about that – and she looked younger than she did in the photo he had given us, but I knew Niddrie was right. We had found our mystery girl.

I smiled at Bruce. 'You did it. Amazing.'

Bruce shrugged. 'I had to go back eight years. She would've been about sixteen or seventeen at the time, but that's all I can tell you. I don't have a name for her. I just take the photos and pass them on to the school. They deal directly with the pupils.'

'That's okay,' I said. 'It gives us something to work on. Can you print out a few copies for me?'

Bruce picked up a brown envelope from his desk and handed it to me. 'Already done that.'

Niddrie turned towards the door.

'Can you wait in the car, Niddrie?' I said. 'I just want a quick word with Bruce.'

'No problem,' he said and left.

I turned to Bruce. 'That must have taken you ages.'

'Not as long as you might think,' he said. 'I concentrated on girls in their last years at school, which narrowed the search. We were just lucky that she was in my files. I'm glad that I was able to help, Allan.'

'How are you, Bruce, and how's your mother?' I asked.

He gave a slight shake of his head.

'I'm okay, but Mum's not great, I'm afraid. She might not have all that long left, if I'm honest.'

'I'm so sorry to hear that,' I said.

After a pause, I went on, 'Look, you're wasted here in Dundee, Bruce. With your talent you could work anywhere. Somewhere you could enjoy life more. Hell, I'm making a right mess of this. Sorry, it's none of my business.'

Bruce smiled ruefully. 'No, I know what you're thinking, Allan. And you're right. I only stayed in Dundee because of Mum. But I'm too old to move now.' He glanced shyly at me. 'Besides, I've met someone.'

'Brilliant! That's brilliant!'

Bruce looked pleased with himself. It was good to see him looking so happy.

'He's a businessman from Edinburgh. We literally bumped into one another in Waterstones – the big book-shop on Commercial Street. He was looking at a collection of photographs and we got talking. It just went on from there. It's been difficult with Mum, but we've managed to spend some time together. And who knows? When the time's right, I might move after all. I like Edinburgh.'

I punched him lightly on the shoulder.

'You sly old dog,' I said. 'Seriously, keep in touch and let me know how things turn out.'

A few minutes later, I got into the car. Niddrie looked over at me.

'He's a poof, isn't he?'

'What makes you think that?'

'We're professional investigators, Allan. At least I am. Trained to spot clues.'

'Hmm, I don't remember giving you any training. All right, Bruce is gay. But he – and I – would prefer it if you kept that to yourself.'

'Fair enough.'

Niddrie paused and looked through the windscreen. 'We had a couple in the Pay Corps. Hardy lads.'

Back in the office we each studied a photo Bruce had given us. Niddrie flicked his with his fingers.

'Well, we now know she did go to school here, which school it was and when she was there. So, how do we move on from there?'

'Actually,' I said. 'The which and the when are a big help. I think I know how we can track her down now. I have a call to make.'

14

Jimmy Russell used to be the chief subeditor of the morning paper I worked on. He's still there and he does pretty much the same job, but he isn't called the chief sub any more. He was given a fancy title about the same time that I stopped being a reporter and became a news gatherer. They gave him a new title but, as he told me, they didn't give him any more money.

I've heard some people – straight out of university and putting in a couple of years as print journalists before trying to get into television – call Jimmy 'old school'. They don't mean it as a compliment. What these clowns don't realise is that Jimmy knows more about journalism than all of them put together.

I learned a lot from Jimmy when I first joined the paper. When I left, I had thanked him for all his help, but he said it was a pleasure to work with someone who listened and didn't think that he already knew all there was to know about being a newspaperman.

We had kept in touch, getting together for a pint now and again. He loved the fact that I had become, in his words, a private dick – a phrase he would repeat in a very loud voice whenever we met. I told him to keep his voice down, in case any nearby ladies overheard and got the wrong idea about the services I was offering.

The first time we had met up, I'd asked him how things were going at work. He said that the lunatics had taken over the asylum. The second time, he said the lunatics were burning the asylum down. The third time, he said that the lunatics were trying to rebuild the asylum, but they had sacked all the bricklayers.

I knew that it was Jimmy's day off, so I called his mobile. 'Fancy a pint?' I asked.

'Let me just check with the forest rangers,' he said. He paused then went on, 'Yep, the good news is that the squirrels are still piddling amongst the trees. I'm in town so meet you in the WAG in ten minutes?'

I said I'd be there and rang off.

Niddrie got to his feet.

'If you don't need me, I'll be off,' he said.

'Okay,' I said. 'I'll let you know how I get on.'

Niddrie left. I didn't ask him where he was going. If he'd wanted me to know, he'd have told me. But I could guess.

When Jimmy walked into the Wig and Gown ten minutes later, I was already sitting at a corner table with two pints of Truman's ESB in front of me. Say what you like about the English, but they do know how to brew a pint. I could almost forgive them for what they did to the Old Steeple . . . but not quite.

Jimmy sat down, picked up his glass and took a long swallow. Then he licked his lips and took a deep breath.

'Ah, I needed that,' he said. 'Thank God you phoned. The wife's been dragging me round shops. I don't even

108

know what she's looking for. I don't think she does either, come to think of it. But she'll know it when she sees it.'

Jimmy took another mouthful of ale.

I knew Jimmy always liked to be asked so I said, 'How're things at the office?'

'There's a quote from one of Shakespeare's plays – can't remember which one. It goes like this: "First, kill all the lawyers." Well, that's out of date. It should be, "First, kill all the HR people, then kill all the lawyers."'

'On top of that, my new editor thinks he's editing *The Times*. We're a provincial newspaper, for fuck's sake. Our readers want stories about what's happening here in Dundee, not Chinese dissidents.'

He sat back and took another sip.

'I've got another couple of years to go. If they made me an offer, I'd go tomorrow, but the miserable bastards won't stump up a penny. They're hoping I'll just quit. So I'm sticking it out. Fuck 'em.'

Now he'd had his usual rant, I knew we could get down to business.

'Jimmy, I'm hoping you can help me with something,' I said.

Jimmy grinned and raised his voice. 'Is this you being a private dick?'

I looked around, but there were no females looking at me hopefully.

'I'm conducting discreet enquiries on behalf of a client,' I said.

'What d'you need to know? Ask away.'

Jimmy had two daughters, now in their twenties. I knew that both had attended the same school in the West End of Dundee that my mystery girl had. So I asked, 'Did you happen to keep Bronagh and Lyndsey's yearbooks from school?'

Jimmy sat back and looked at me, his mouth slightly agape. 'Well, I wasn't expecting you to ask me that.'

I showed Jimmy the photo Bruce had given me.

'I'm trying to trace this girl. I know that she was at the same school as your girls at about the same time, but I don't know her name. School yearbooks always have photos of all the classes with the pupils' names printed underneath them.'

Jimmy finished his pint. 'Bronagh never throws anything out. The book you want is bound to be in the house some-where. Come by tonight and I should have it for you. Say about eight?'

'Thanks, Jimmy. I really appreciate this.'

We both stood.

'I'd love to have another, but I'd better go,' said Jimmy. 'I told the wife I'd only be about half an hour. She shouldn't have done too much damage to the credit card in that time. See you tonight.'

Jimmy had owned the same house in the West End of the city for nearly thirty years. It was a solid stone-built affair with high ceilings and original features throughout. He steadfastly refused to modernise it, which meant it was draughty and the roof needed new slates after every winter. It was the kind of house I would have loved to live in.

There were quite a few houses like it in Dundee and across the river in Newport. Jimmy had done a bit of research and found out that it had been built by one of the men who managed the mills on behalf of the jute barons.

My granddad once told me that while those jute barons were playing the philanthropist, their managers were mean bastards who made sure the owners got their money's worth out of the poor sods who worked in the mills – like my great grandparents. It had cost less than £500 nearly 150 years ago. If Jimmy ever decided to sell, he would be looking for nearly 900 times that. Which meant I wouldn't be buying it.

At 8 p.m. on the dot I rapped the brass knocker twice. Seconds later, Jimmy opened the door.

'Come on in, Allan,' he said. He led the way into a small room, which he used as his study. The walls were lined with bookcases, and in the centre of the room was a small table with a bottle of malt whisky and two glasses on it. Also on the table was a small pile of school yearbooks. A couple of old leather armchairs faced each other across the table.

We sat. Jimmy picked up the bottle and looked at me quizzically.

'You know I don't drink whisky, Jimmy,' I said. 'Besides, I'm driving.'

He poured himself a glass.

'Fair enough,' he said. 'But you won't mind if I do.'

Jimmy indicated the yearbooks.

'Bronagh and her sister are living in Edinburgh now, but I looked in her old room and found them under the bed. I told you she was a hoarder. Help yourself.'

I had a good idea of which year I should be looking at. I flicked through the book, scanning the rows of young faces. There she was, in the class photo of 5B2, third from the left in the second row – Mary Pigott, alias Tina Lamont.

As Jimmy sipped his malt I looked through the rest of the book. There was one other reference to Mary, in a section where the leaving class discussed their dreams and ambitions.

Mary hadn't actually written anything about herself, but another girl called Stacey Watson had been quoted saying she hoped that Mary would still speak to them when she was a dancer in a smash-hit musical on the West End stage. I guessed that she was talking about the one in London. There is a stage in the West End of Dundee, but it's in a converted cinema. You can see a show there, but it will be a production put on by one of the local musical societies. This could have been why Mary had gone to London. I know a clue when it jumps up and hits me in the face.

I closed the book and laid it back on the table.

'Found her then?' asked Jimmy.

'Yeah, I did. Thanks again, Jimmy. You've been a big help.'

As Jimmy showed me out he said, 'Let me know how it all turns out. I might be able to include it in my memoirs.'

'You're writing your memoirs?'

He gave me an evil grin. 'Oh, yeah. That's one good thing about not getting a deal to leave. I'd have to have signed a non-disclosure agreement. I know a lot of dirty secrets about a lot of dirty bastards.'

15

I texted Niddrie to tell him what I had found out from my visit to Jimmy Russell. The next morning, he appeared at the office just as I was unlocking the door.

We sat down and he looked at me expectantly.

'Her name is Mary Pigott – one "g" and two "t"s,' I said. 'I checked the phone book. It's an unusual spelling of the name. There are only two numbers for a Pigott with that spelling in the local directory and only one of them is in the catchment area for the school she attended. So, it shouldn't be too difficult to track her down now.'

Niddrie looked thoughtful for a moment. 'There's something weird about this. When you compared Mary's school photo to the one Carter gave us, you said it was obvious that she's a lot older in the latter. So why is she wearing a school uniform when she's an adult? And why is that the only photo his client has of her? Some kind of kinky stuff going on?'

'Our job's to find her, not judge her,' I said. 'The name in the phone book is a Mr C. Pigott. That could be her father. Let's see if there's a Mary Pigott listed at the same address.'

After a few minutes online, I found a Mr Colin Pigott and a Mrs Irene Pigott at the address, but no Mary.

'Could still be her parents,' I said. 'I think we should

check it out. If I'm right, they could tell us where she is now.'

Niddie did not share my enthusiasm; he looked concerned, his eyebrows furrowed. 'But if they are Mary's folks, they might not know that their grown-up daughter has been dressing up as a schoolgirl and that some guy from London is looking for her. I don't think we can just go barging in. Maybe we should do a reconnaissance first.'

'You mean like you used to do in the Pay Corps?' I said.

'Exactly. Many's the time I had to do a quick recce before handing out the wage packets.'

'Okay,' I said. 'Let's take a look.'

The Pigotts lived on a small estate not far from Jimmy Russell's house. However, while I would have loved to have lived in a house like Jimmy's, you couldn't have paid me enough to live in a house like the Pigotts'.

The estate was built in the seventies – not a decade associated with creative design in house building in Dundee, or just about anywhere else. The architect had obviously had a fixation with boxes, and the builder had crammed as many houses onto the piece of land as he could get away with. There were 'FOR SALE' signs in front of some of the houses, but they looked as if they'd been up for some time.

The Pigotts' house was a bungalow. I've seen bigger kennels, but it was obviously cared for. The front lawn was tiny, but the grass was carefully trimmed and someone had taken time over the planting of the flowerbed in its centre. The wooden window frames appeared freshly painted and there was a paved driveway up the side of the house. An elderly Corsa looked as if it was having a well-earned rest there.

I stopped about twenty yards from the Pigotts' driveway on the other side of the street. We sat for an hour but there was no sign of any movement from the house. In fact, there was no sign of any movement on the whole estate.

'You know what this reminds me of?' I asked. 'One of those movies where nearly everyone on earth has been turned into a zombie and whole cities have been abandoned.'

'And here was me thinking you only watched old films with tragic heroines and heroes with stiff upper lips.'

'Ailsa dragged me to one. Okay, we've carried out a reconnaissance; now it's time to go barging in.'

'You're better at barging in than I am,' said Niddrie. 'I'll wait here. But if I see you being attacked by zombies, I'll call for help.'

I rang the front doorbell. A few seconds later, the door opened a few inches, held by a security chain. In the gap I could see half a woman's face. She was in her fifties and she looked like Mary would after one of those age progression makeovers.

I tried my best smile.

'My name's Linton. I'm trying to trace a Mary Pigott. I believe this is her address.'

'You're mistaken. There's no Mary Pigott here.'

The door slammed shut and I could hear a lock clicking. It's hard to take when even your best smile can't open doors for you.

I went back to the car and reported to Niddrie. 'The woman who answered the door said there was no Mary Pigott there, but one thing's for sure. She's Mary's mum. The likeness was unmistakable.'

115

'So, what do we do now?'

'We wait and talk to Colin Pigott. He could be at work. Maybe he'll be a bit more helpful.'

There was no point in hanging about, so we went and had lunch. There are lots of little cafes and coffee shops in the West End serving dainty little sandwiches and about thirty different types of fair trade tea, so we went to a bakery and bought pies and cans of a fizzy drink that was reputedly made from girders. Actually, I don't think the makers can advertise it as such nowadays, since some killjoy complained that it wasn't totally accurate. I mean, really?

Magdalen Green is Dundee's oldest public park. It has a fine view overlooking the River Tay to the west of the railway bridge. The locals have been taking the air and enjoying that view for more than four hundred years, in between wars and invasions. Luckily, the only sign of violence we spotted when we parked the car was two seagulls fighting over a slice of bread, so we decided it was safe to sit on a bench and eat.

My granddad taught me how to eat a Dundee pie. There's a little hole in the top of the pastry case, and he had told me to turn the pie upside down and let all the grease run out. It took a couple of minutes, but it could extend your life expectancy by up to three days. My granddad offered no actual medical research to back up this claim, but he lived into his nineties and ate pies every week, apart from the five years he had spent – and I quote – 'sorting out that wee bastard Hitler'. I think he had had some help with that one.

Obviously, Niddrie hadn't had anyone to pass on tips for a healthy diet. He took a big bite out of his pie then looked over at me as the last of the grease from my pie dribbled onto the grass at my feet.

'What are you doing?' he asked.

'Just prolonging my life. You go ahead and risk cardiac arrest. I did a first aid course about ten years ago. I think I remember some of it.'

We washed the pies down with the liquidised girders. As we had been rendered incapable of movement for the foreseeable future, it seemed a good opportunity to discuss the case.

'Mrs Pigott said that there was no Mary living at the house, but she didn't deny that she had a daughter called Mary. Why? Either she genuinely doesn't know where Mary is, or she does and wouldn't tell me.'

'I think she must know,' said Niddrie. 'If you had no idea where your daughter was and some guy came to your door saying he was looking for her, wouldn't you at least want to talk to him about it – find out what he knew?'

'You're right. Let's hope that I get the chance to explain to her dad that I don't want to cause any trouble for Mary. If she doesn't want to speak to Carter, that's up to her.' I looked at my watch. 'If Mr Pigott has been at work, he might come home in the next hour or so. Let's go back to the house.'

We parked in the same spot as before. I wouldn't say the place had come alive, but a few kids sauntered up the street on their way home from school. I wondered if that had been Mary just a few years ago, and what had happened to her since.

The kids didn't pay any attention to us. Most were speaking or texting on their phones, probably to classmates they had left just minutes before. One thing they all had in common was that they carried enormous backpacks. I'd once seen a photograph of my granddad just before he invaded

Sicily. He'd had less on his back when he had gone to sort out that wee bastard than those kids carried to school every day.

Just before 5 p.m., a van turned into the Pigotts' driveway. Lettered on the sides were the words 'PIGOTT PLUMBERS' and a mobile phone number. A man in his fifties wearing a dark-green sweatshirt with PP embroidered on the chest got out and went into the house. We waited ten minutes, and then went up to the door.

It opened before I knocked, all the way this time, and a grim-faced Mr Pigott confronted us. His wife stood just behind him.

I could see my best smile wasn't going to work on him either, so I quickly said, 'Mr Pigott? My name's Allan Linton. I'm a private investigator and I'm trying to get in touch with your daughter on behalf of a client.'

'We've nothing to say to you. Please leave now.'

'Look, I know this may seem strange to you, but I assure you I mean Mary no harm. I won't tell anyone where she is without her permission.'

Pigott leaned forward. He was barely keeping his temper in check. 'You harassed my wife and now you're harassing me. Get off my property now or I'll call the police.'

I backed off, raising my hands in surrender. 'I apologise. I won't bother you again.'

Pigott slammed the door and I walked back down the drive, past the Corsa and the van. Niddrie followed. As he passed the little car, he bent down. I thought he was tying his shoelace.

Once we were back in the car, I shook my head. 'They know where she is, I'm sure of it. But how do we get them to tell us?'

'Actually, I think they may lead us right to her,' said Niddrie. 'While you were distracting them, I was looking for clues.'

I waited, but Niddrie was at his irritating worst. Finally, I asked, 'And I suppose you found some?'

'I did. Take a look at the Corsa and tell me what you see.'

I turned and looked at the old car.

'Well, it's ten years old and it looks like it could do with a good wash.'

'Exactly. It looks like it's been driven through mud, but it hasn't rained here for days and the roads are dry. There's no way it could have got in that state just driving round the city. Looks to me like it's been driven on a muddy track.'

'But it could've been dirty like that for days,' I said.

'Don't think so. Look at the state of the house and the garden. They're immaculate. People who keep their property tidy usually keep their cars clean too. I reckon that wee car has been in the countryside in the last day or two. Then there's this.'

Niddrie held up a forefinger. There was something dark stuck to the nail.

'Horseshit,' he said.

'I know I'm being slow on the uptake, but there's no need to be insulting.'

Niddrie sighed and raised his finger closer to my face.

'No, this is horse shit.'

'How do you know that?'

Niddrie gave me a look.

'I spent a few months in a place where a lot of the transport is still horse-drawn. I've stepped in enough of it. That's how I know. I scraped it out of the tread on one of the tyres when I bent down beside the car. When was the last time you saw a horse crapping in the street in Dundee? That settles it, as far as I'm concerned. The Pigotts have driven out of town in the last couple of days. Now, it could be they were just out for a wee drive, or visiting friends. Or it could be they went to see Mary –'

'Who lives at the end of a muddy track which has horses nearby. Well, there's one way to find out for certain. We have to keep an eye on that car and follow it next time it leaves the house.'

If you use just one car to tail someone, then there's a good chance that the person being followed will eventually notice it, even if it's as nondescript as a small Hyundai. We needed another vehicle, so we drove to a car hire depot and I rented a small white van for Niddrie. I wasn't being stingy – after all, Carter said he would meet all reasonable expenses – but who pays any attention to a small white van? There must be hundreds in the Dundee area alone.

Obviously, the Pigotts would have noticed a strange vehicle parked outside their house all day, but there was only one road leading in and out of their estate. All we had to do was to take it in turns to park close to the junction where it joined the main road and wait. If one of us spotted the Corsa on the move, we could use our mobiles to call the other. I had a hands-free kit installed in my car and I gave my spare one to Niddrie.

I took the first watch but by 11 p.m. I reckoned that the Pigotts were in for the night, so I called Niddrie and told him he could stand down. He said he would be in place by 7 a.m. the next morning, and I went home to bed.

This went on for a couple of days. We saw Mr Pigott

leave for work about 8 a.m. and return about 5 p.m. Niddrie remarked that his van never appeared to be particularly dirty. The Corsa seemed to be for Mrs Pigott's use. She did leave the house three times – once to go to a butcher's shop, another to take the Corsa though a car wash and once more, finally, to visit a large supermarket. But none of the trips involved driving down muddy tracks and she never went near a horse, unless the butcher knew something he wasn't telling.

It was on the third morning as I was finishing breakfast that I got a call from Niddrie. 'She's on the move. She's heading west, towards the road to Perth.'

That was the opposite end of the city.

'Be with you as soon as I can. Keep in touch.'

I was in my car and heading west when Niddrie called again.

'She's not going to Perth. She's joined the Kingsway and is now heading east.'

The Kingsway is Dundee's ring road; all along its length, roads lead off north into the countryside. Niddrie called again.

'She's at the traffic lights at the junction with Forfar Road. She's signalling to turn left.'

'I'm not far away. Be behind you soon.'

Five minutes later, I saw the white van. The Corsa was a hundred yards in front, a couple of vehicles ahead. They were doing about fifty miles an hour on the dual carriage-way to Forfar. I overtook the van and Niddrie dropped back a bit, until there was a truck between us.

We kept swapping positions until the Corsa signalled left and turned onto a B road. This meant things got a bit trickier; there was a lot less traffic on the road, making it easier for Mrs Pigott to spot us.

However, the road was narrow, with a lot of sharp bends. I reckoned she was too busy concentrating on her driving to pay much attention to her rear-view mirror.

After about twenty minutes, she signalled again and made a sudden turn, catching me unawares. Niddrie was in front of me, but both of us held back. Mrs Pigott turned onto a muddy track, which ended in front of a cottage about a hundred yards off the road. We both drove past the turn-off and pulled into a layby with a gravel surface. We were screened from the cottage by a line of trees. There didn't seem to be any signs of life at the cottage. Had she spotted us tailing her and led us to a dead end?

I took a pair of binoculars out of my glove box and joined Niddrie, who was already out of the van and peering through the trees.

'Look,' he said, and I followed his pointing finger. Fields lined the track and in one of them were two horses. 'Now we know where she picked up the horse shit. She's been here before.'

I focused the binoculars on the Corsa, which was parked outside the cottage's front door. Mrs Pigott was taking a couple of large plastic shopping bags out of the boot. The door of the cottage opened and I turned my binoculars on it.

A young woman came out. Her hair wasn't long and it wasn't blonde. It was short and dark, but I still recognised her.

We had found Mary Pigott.

16

Mary helped her mother carry the shopping bags into the cottage then closed the door. I looked at Niddrie.

'You got it spot on,' I said.

'The signs were there. You just had to read them right. What do we do now?'

I thought for a moment.

'Mary went to a lot of trouble to make sure she wasn't found. Now, maybe she just wants to be left alone, or maybe there's another reason. Whatever it is, if we go and speak to her now, she might just disappear again. It was hard enough finding her this time; I don't want to go through all that again.

'We know where she is at the moment and, if her mum's taking in a load of shopping, it's reasonable to assume that she'll be staying there for the next few days at least. We can take turns driving past a couple of times a day to make sure she's staying put. I'm expecting Carter to phone again in the next day or two. When he does, I'll tell him we've found Mary but I won't tell him where. He can give me a message to pass on to her, and then we'll go and speak to her. It's up to her whether or not she agrees to meet him – or his client. But, as far as we're concerned, we'll have done what we said we would.'

'And he can pay the rest of our fee,' Niddrie added. 'Sounds good to me. I'll check on Mary this evening and every evening till you hear from Carter. You can take the mornings. If anything happens one can call the other.'

I let Niddrie drive off first, then waited half an hour before I turned the car and headed back to Dundee. The Corsa was still parked outside the cottage when I left.

I had the Beatles' album *Please Please Me* in the CD player, and I listened to it all the way back into Dundee. My dad was fifteen when it was released, and he said the first time he heard 'Twist and Shout', it was like being kicked in the stomach. He could hardly breathe. My breathing remained steady as the track came on, but a big grin spread over my face. Oh, I know that McCartney and Lennon wrote some of the greatest songs of the last century but, as far as my dad is concerned, nothing beats 'Twist and Shout'. And that's one they didn't write. Two guys called Phil Medley and Bert Berns deserve the credit for that.

The song was actually written in 1961, and there were two recordings before the Beatles' version. I've listened to both. The first, by two American guys called the Top Notes, is done in a corny Latin American rhythm and it's dire. Hard to believe anyone could ruin 'Twist and Shout', but somehow they managed it.

The second, by the Isley Brothers, isn't so bad. The Isleys made some great recordings, but 'Twist and Shout' isn't one of them. Let's just say no one would have trouble breathing after hearing it.

But then came George Harrison's jerky, clunking guitar, Ringo Starr's driving combination of snare and bass drums and an absolute masterclass in bass guitar lines from the much-maligned Paul McCartney. And on top of all that,

John Lennon's searing vocal, to finish off one of the greatest rock and roll performances of all time.

My dad saw the band play at the Caird Hall in Dundee in the early sixties. He is always emphatic that he saw them, but couldn't hear them for all the screaming. He is still seriously pissed off about that, even after all these years.

But, as the decade wore on, Dad's dedication to the Beatles faltered. He hated the drugs, the women and that weird guy – the maha-something-or-other. It finally died with 'Hey Jude'. He told me he listened to about thirty seconds then took the disc off his record player and threw it in the bin. Now, I know to some people that is sacrilege, but listen to 'Twist and Shout', then 'Hey Jude'. Which one gets you moving your whole body and which makes you wonder if there's a sharp razor blade in easy reach?

I parked the car and went up to the office. I thought I'd better check my answer machine to see if anyone had called.

As I climbed the last flight of stairs, I heard someone knocking on the door of my office. There, turning away from the door, was a woman. And she did something even The Beatles couldn't: she took my breath away.

17

It wasn't that she was classically beautiful, and to describe her as simply "attractive" would have been completely wrong. "Striking" was the first word to come to my mind, closely followed by "intriguing". Maybe her mouth was a little too wide and her nose a little long, but the combination somehow worked perfectly.

Her eyes were hooded so that she seemed to tilt her head back when she looked at me; as our eyes met, I saw that hers were a deep green. Her face was framed by glossy, dark-brown hair, which gently curled in on either side of her chin. I put her age at about forty. And the sum total of all these parts? She was as sexy as hell.

I finally managed to get my breathing back under control. 'Can I help you?' I asked.

She opened her mouth to reveal even white teeth, and when she spoke I thought I detected a faint accent, though I couldn't place it.

'I'm looking for Mr Allan Linton,' she said.

Time to try my best smile again.

'I'm Allan Linton. And you are . . .?'

This time the smile worked. Her expression softened and she smiled back. 'My name's Morrison.'

I recognised the name, but it took me a second to remember why.

'Are you by any chance related to the old lady who wrote to me about her missing cat?'

She looked puzzled for a moment, then she laughed.

'I *am* the old lady who wrote to you about my missing cat. I'm Danielle Morrison. Why did you think I'd be an old lady?'

I shook my head ruefully. 'In this day and age no one writes letters like that any more. It was just so beautifully written – the style, the grammar, the penmanship. I'm afraid I jumped to conclusions. I'm sorry.'

She smiled again.

'Don't apologise. The English language is beautiful and should be treated with such respect.' She made a dismissive gesture with her hand and went on, 'I use all the modern devices like everyone else, but I love to write a letter when I can. I even took a course in calligraphy. But I think the personal touch is even better, don't you agree? So, when I found myself in the area, I thought I'd come to your office.'

She tilted her head back. There was a hint of wickedness in her expression.

'That is, if you have an office, and not just your name on a door.'

Was that a hint?

'Oh, I have an office. Please, come in.'

I unlocked the office door and gestured her to the client seat, then sat down facing her. That was no hardship at all.

'I wanted to thank you,' she said. 'I took your advice and put up posters where I live. Only a day later some children called me. They'd found Sacha. Now he's home safe with me again.'

Lucky bastard, I thought.

'I'm pleased to have been some help.'

She looked earnestly at me. 'You must let me repay you in some way.'

Before my imagination ran away with me, I managed to blurt out, 'No, that's absolutely not necessary.'

'Are you sure?'

That's when my detective training kicked in. She had signed the letter Miss D. Morrison. From that, I managed to work out she wasn't actually married. True, there could have been a partner or a boyfriend but, if there was, he hadn't been much use in finding Sacha, had he? Just to confirm my suspicions, I took a quick look at her left hand. No ring. So, I took the plunge.

'There is one thing you could do for me, Miss Morrison. You could agree to have dinner with me.'

I held my breath, but she grinned and said, 'I'd love to. And call me Dani, please.' She reached over my desk and picked up a pen and writing pad. 'Shall we say this Saturday? Here's my number. Call me. I look forward to it.'

After I had escorted her out of my office, I shut the door with a self-satisfied sigh. The day wasn't turning out too badly. We had finally tracked down Mary, which meant I would receive the remainder of my fee – which in turn meant I could spend some time thinking of somewhere special to take Dani.

There was no message from Carter on my answer machine, so I decided to call it a day and go home.

A couple of hours later, I was finishing up my dinner.

Years ago, when I was just a young reporter, I read a lot of

American crime fiction. To this day, no crime authors have surpassed Ed McBain or Elmore Leonard in my eyes – both, sadly, no longer writing great crime stories featuring some truly unforgettable characters. A few have come close. One such contender wrote a series of novels featuring a private eye who was also an expert in the kitchen. There were whole passages in the books describing the hero chopping, season-ing, marinating and cooking, when he wasn't gunning down the bad guys. I didn't do any of that when cooking, especially not the gunning down part. I grilled some chops, boiled some potatoes and added a mixed salad I'd bought in the supermarket. The only seasoning came from the cruet set.

Afterwards, I sat on the couch, but before I could switch on the TV, my mobile phone rang. It was Niddrie.

'Where are you?' he asked.

'Here in my flat.'

'Switch on Sky News.'

I clicked the remote till the news channel came up. A blonde reporter was describing how a judge had been found dead in a flat in London. In the background, a 'Police Do Not Cross' tape was tied across the entrance to a block of flats. I'm not familiar with the London property market, but it didn't look like a council tenement.

The reporter was saying that the police had not yet released details of how the judge had died, but they were treating it as an unlawful killing. Apparently the victim had been the judge in some very high-profile trials. As she spoke, a photo of the judge in his robe and wig appeared on the screen. It was captioned 'Judge Bernard Tavernier'.

I stared at the television. I knew the man, but not as Bernard Tavernier. When he came into my office and hired me to find Mary Pigott, he had called himself Carter.

18

By the time Niddrie and I met in my office the following morning, more details of Tavernier's death had emerged. The police were still trying to find out who owned the flat where he had been found. The early morning news showed footage of his house where he had lived with his wife, Caroline, in a little village called Potten End in Hertfordshire. A solicitor came on camera to say that the family would not be giving interviews and had asked for their privacy to be respected.

Tavernier had had a reputation for handing down lengthy sentences to some nasty criminals. Speculation had already begun that one of them had been looking for revenge. There were other reports that his death was the result of a robbery gone wrong, and that his wallet, phone and expensive watch were missing. But no one was specifying the exact cause of death yet. That didn't surprise me. From my time covering crimes, I knew that they would still be carrying out the autopsy. The police were appealing for anyone with information to contact them.

'Do we go to the cops and tell them what we know?' asked Niddrie.

'What do we know? That he came here and hired us to look for someone on behalf of a client and that he gave us a false name. Remember, he insisted we keep it strictly confidential, so there could be an issue with client/lawyer confidentiality.'

'Hold on,' said Niddrie. 'He wasn't just some lawyer; he was a judge. I'm no legal expert, but I don't think that judges act on behalf of clients. And then there's the photograph of Mary he gave us ... a grown woman dressed like some naughty schoolgirl? There's something not right here, Allan.'

I sighed, mulling it over. 'Okay, but his death could still have nothing to do with him hiring us to find Mary Pigott. You heard what they've been saying on the news. It could've been a robbery or some thug with a grudge. Mary Pigott obviously has her own reasons for not wanting to be found. If we go to the police, she'll be dragged into it. I think we should go and tell her about Tavernier wanting to find her. She might tell us why. If it has nothing to do with Tavernier's death, we can let the whole thing drop. Let's face it, we have no way of contacting his client. We don't even know who he is. In fact, we don't even know if there ever was a client.'

'Right, but we don't hang about," said Niddrie. 'We go and see Mary Pigott now. If there's anything dodgy going on, we speak to the cops.'

We took my car. An hour later we pulled up at the cottage where we had first seen Mary. When she opened the door, I noticed she looked tired. That wasn't surprising; she had a small child in her arms.

'Mary, isn't it?' I said, trying to sound amiable. 'My name's Allan Linton. I'm a private investigator and' – I gestured behind me – 'this is my colleague, Niddrie.'

Mary took a step back. I'm sure she would have slammed

the door, but that's kind of difficult with a baby in your arms, so I quickly added, 'Mary, we mean you no harm, and I promise you we won't tell anyone where you live without your permission. We just want to ask you a few questions.'

'You're the ones who went to my mum and dad's house, aren't you? You don't give up, do you?' She sighed and rolled her eyes heavenwards. 'All right, you've got ten minutes.'

She led the way into a small sitting room. A threadbare couch, flanked by two matching armchairs, faced an open fire in which a couple of big logs were burning down. A little wooden chest acted as a coffee table. The furniture was old-fashioned, but solid and well cared for. I remember – from when Ailsa was a baby – how difficult it is to keep a place tidy when there's a child in the house. It looked to me like Mary was making a pretty good job of it. Her child was asleep in some kind of romper suit and I couldn't tell if it was a girl or a boy. I guessed he or she was a few weeks old, well fed and contented.

Mary sat in one of the armchairs and I took the one opposite. Niddrie eased himself down onto the couch. Mary looked at me and raised an eyebrow. An invitation to start talking.

'A man calling himself Carter hired us on behalf of a client to find a woman called Tina Lamont,' I explained. 'All we had to go on was a photo and his belief she came from Dundee. He never told us why his client wanted to trace Tina. He said it was strictly confidential.'

I took the photo of Tina Lamont out of my pocket and showed it to Mary. She took a few moments to study it, and then looked up at me again. Her face was impassive.

'This is you, isn't it?'

She shrugged.

I went on, 'I won't bore you with the whole story, but we had a bit of luck and managed to identify the girl in the photo as you. Our agreement with Carter was that, if we found you, we would pass on a message to you. Then you could decide if you wanted to meet him. But we haven't been able to do that. You see, Carter wasn't his real name. His real name was Bernard Tavernier and he was a judge in London. He was found dead in a flat there yesterday.'

I looked Mary in the eye, but there was no reaction at the mention of Tavernier's name. I glanced over at Niddrie. He was slumped on the couch, looking very comfortable, so I didn't disturb him.

'It's been on the news; maybe you saw it?' I asked.

'I don't bother with the news.' Mary directed my attention towards her child with nod of her head. 'This one keeps me busy.'

'We just want to make sure that his death has nothing to do with our search for you. Have you any idea why Tavernier was looking for you? I understand you went to London to become a dancer. Maybe you came across him – or his client – while you lived there?'

That got her attention.

'You know about my being a dancer? I'm impressed. If I ever need a private detective, I'll know who to come to.'

I looked into Mary's eyes again. They had hardened. Mary was a new mum and could only have been in her early twenties, but she looked like she wouldn't take any crap from anyone, let alone me. I moved on before she told me to get lost and to take Niddrie with me.

'So,' I started tentatively, 'do you know Tavernier? Er, maybe you came across him in court?'

'You mean, did I commit any crime?'

133

'No,' I said hastily. 'Maybe as a witness?'

Mary shook her head. I could see the baby was starting to wake up.

'No, I don't remember ever meeting him.'

'What about the photo? Do you recall it being taken? And why did he say your name was Tina Lamont?'

Mary looked down at her child then back up at me.

'When I lived in London, I went to a few parties. A couple of them were fancy dress. I think I hired a schoolgirl costume for one of them. I was invited by a girl I worked with. It was just a bit of fun. There were lots of people there. Maybe this client was one of them and he took the picture, but I've no idea why he thought my name was Tina Lamont. Maybe he got me mixed up with some other girl. There was always a lot of alcohol at these parties – not to mention drugs.' She looked at me defiantly. 'I never did any drugs.'

I looked thoughtfully back at her.

'You know, it wasn't easy to find you,' I said. 'First, we had the wrong name. Then, when we did manage to identify you, your parents weren't exactly helpful.'

'Like I said, I've no idea why anyone thought my name was Tina whatever. As for my mum and dad, they're just being protective. They don't want anyone bothering me.'

She gazed down at the baby. He or she was making burbling noises.

'It's time for his feed,' she said pointedly.

'One last question,' said Niddrie, piping up from his spot on the couch. 'Why did you come back from London?'

Mary looked pityingly at Niddrie, then addressed me. 'Is he kidding? It's hard enough trying to get work as a dancer down there as it is. It's bloody impossible when you have a baby.'

Niddrie pursed his lips before speaking again. 'I can see that, but what about the boy's father? Couldn't he have helped out? Maybe he still could.'

I could see where Niddrie was going with this, but so could Mary. She turned back to Niddrie, her face twisted.

'Oh, I see what you're driving at. You think this mysterious client could be my son's father, who now wants to do the right thing by me. Well, you've got that all wrong. He made it perfectly clear he wanted nothing to do with my son or me. Not that it's any of your business. Look, I've answered all your questions. I haven't lived in London for ages and I don't know anything about this judge guy or his client. I'd appreciate it if you left my family alone. They've had a hard enough time dealing with me coming home and having a baby.'

I stood up and Niddrie followed, easing himself up from the couch.

'Thanks for answering our questions,' I said. 'We'll see ourselves out.'

A few moments later we looked at each other over the top of my car.

'Well?' said Niddrie.

'I need time to think,' I replied. 'Let's go back to the office and we'll discuss it.'

Forty-five minutes later, I was at my desk. Niddrie sat where Dani had been less than twenty-four hours before. Back then, I had been feeling pretty pleased with myself. I'd had a lot to look forward to, including picking up another five grand. I know that on television and in thrillers the private detectives don't ever seem to be worried about getting paid.

Well, as much as I like to solve the mystery, I like to be rewarded for my labours even more – in cash, preferably.

With just the slimmest of clues, we had followed the trail right to Mary Pigott, only for it to peter out at her cottage.

I had thought about it all the way back to Dundee and up into my office, where Niddrie and I continued to sit and think in silence. I could have saved myself all that thinking. I had known from the start that there were only two choices.

'Either we go to the police or we don't,' I said.

Niddrie looked at me and sighed.

'It only took you three-quarters of an hour to work that out? No wonder you get paid the big bucks and I'm just the associate.'

'You're my most valued member of staff,' I said.

'I'm your only member of staff.'

'Okay, let's say we go to the police. What can we tell them? That we met Tavernier only once and he gave us a false name? But we don't know why he did it. We didn't even find out who he really was till we saw the news.'

I remembered what Niddrie had asked Mary just before we left the cottage.

'Tavernier said he was representing a client, but we've absolutely no idea if he was or not. Your assumption that the client could be the father of Mary's son was reasonable, but I believed her when she said there was no chance of that. We found the girl in the photo Tavernier gave us. He was correct when he said she was from Dundee. But the photo is the only real link between Mary and Tavernier, and Mary Pigott is positive she doesn't know him. And she did come up with a perfectly plausible explanation as to why he had her photo.'

Niddrie nodded, listening.

I leaned back in my chair and continued, 'True, she was hard to find, but I don't believe she was deliberately trying to cover her tracks. Tavernier told us his client thought her name was Tina Lamont. That could be because, as Mary said, someone at the party got her mixed up with another girl and gave Tavernier's client the wrong name. Easily done after a few drinks or some recreational drug-taking.'

I looked over to check Niddrie hadn't drifted off. He looked semi-alert, so I carried on.

'This is the way I see it. During her time in London, Mary went to this party. Some guy saw her there and took her picture on his phone. But that must have been some time ago. Mary said she hasn't lived in London for ages and she sure doesn't look pregnant in the photo. So, for whatever reason, this guy decides he wants to get in touch with Mary now. It happens. There was a story in the papers a few weeks ago about some bloke who met a girl on a plane, was too shy to ask her for a date, and then spent weeks trying to find her.'

'I remember that,' said Niddrie. 'Didn't work out too well. He found her in the end, but it turned out she'd been on her way to get married . . . to her long-term girlfriend. So why didn't this guy come looking for Mary himself? Why all the secrecy?'

'Lots of reasons. He could be married. Whatever it is, he asks Tavernier to help find her. Remember, Tavernier told us he had connections to someone in the legal profession in Dundee.'

Niddrie thought for a moment, then said, 'Fair enough, but why did Tavernier give us a fake name? And why did he offer us so much money to find Mary?'

'Bernard Tavernier isn't the most common name. He

probably thought that if we knew who he really was, we'd start asking questions. As for the fee ... Well, as I said, the client may have had good reasons for keeping the whole thing quiet. And he might be rich enough to afford laying out a few grand.'

Niddrie looked thoughtful but said nothing.

'Mary left London a long time ago,' I added. 'She says she has never met Tavernier and she doesn't know who took the photo. She's obviously just trying to get on with her life now. I'd hate to screw things up for her. If we gave her name to the police, she could get caught up in an investiga-tion-into a crime that took place five hundred miles away and has nothing to do with her.'

I thought suddenly of Bruce McAllister. If we went to the police, they'd want to know how we found Mary, and his name would come up. I knew he'd freak out if the police wanted to interview him. I made up my mind.

'Look,' I said, 'before we went to see Mary, I said that if our search for her had nothing to do with Tavernier's death, we should let the whole thing drop. Given what we know now, I think that's what we should do.'

Niddrie nodded and stood up. 'Well, I guess that's the end of this case then. Anything else you need a hand with?'

'Not at the moment, I'm sorry to say. But you know what this business is like – we could be run off our feet next week.'

Niddrie went to the door, stopped and looked back. There was that ripple in his cheek muscle again.

'Till then I'll remain in a state of high alert. See you.'

19

Occasionally, when I successfully conclude a case, I feel elated. Satisfied by a job well done. Indeed, initially, I'd been really pleased that we had managed to trace Tina/Mary. But now I felt like I had reached the last few pages of a novel, only to find that someone had ripped them out. I guessed I would never find out why Tavernier had come to me just a few days ago.

True, we had completed the task that Tavernier had set us and, strictly speaking, I could present an invoice for £5000, plus expenses, to the executors of his estate for services rendered. However, there was one slight problem: I didn't have any actual proof that Tavernier had hired me. Somehow, I didn't see them saying no problem, before asking if I preferred cheque or cash.

Normally, I write a report when I finish a job. I pass one on to the client and keep a copy for my files. This time, I would make just the one copy, but I didn't feel like starting on it now.

I looked at the school photo of Ailsa on my desk, then checked my watch. She would be coming out of school. If I hurried, I could meet her. That would improve my mood.

But I didn't have to wait until I met Ailsa before my

day got better. I ran out of my office building, turned sharply right and almost knocked someone over. It was a woman and, as she fell backwards, I grabbed her by the shoulders. A pair of deep-green hooded eyes looked up into mine.

'You're obviously in a hurry, Allan. Don't let me hold you back.'

'Dani! I'm so sorry. Are you all all right?'

She straightened up. 'I'm perfectly fine. Off you go then. You obviously have a very important appointment to keep.'

'What? No, it's okay. I don't have any appointments. I've finished work for today. You weren't coming to see me by any chance, were you?'

'No, I've also just finished work and I've a few things to do before going home.'

'Actually, I was going to call you this evening about Saturday. What kind of food do you fancy? I'll book a table.'

Dani frowned.

'No, don't do that,' she said.

I panicked. Had she changed her mind?

'There's a little restaurant near where I live,' Dani continued. 'It's nothing special, but the food's very good.'

'Nothing special' sounded perfect. That normally meant 'not expensive', which I was relieved to hear, especially when I thought of the five grand I wasn't going to receive. And she still wanted to have dinner with me. I tried to hide the relief on my face … and failed miserably.

Dani smiled.

'Oh, did you think I'd changed my mind? No, Allan, I'm still looking forward to having dinner with you. It's an Italian restaurant. Is that okay?'

I'd have been happy to have dinner with Dani in some greasy spoon.

'I like Italian,' I said. 'I'll pick you up, say around eight?'

That smile again.

'No, that's all right. I'll meet you there. It's called Vincenzo's; it's on the Perth Road.'

As Dani walked off, she glanced back at me.

'I'll book the table. See you Saturday at eight.'

I stood there, a soppy grin still spread across my face, when I realised there was somebody beside me. I turned to find Ailsa smiling up at me.

'Hi, Dad.'

'Oh, hi. I was just coming to see if you fancied going for a coffee.'

'Sorry, Dad. I have a ton of homework. I'm going to Mum's office to work there.'

'Oh, that's okay. Another time.'

Ailsa tilted her head and looked at me sideways. A knowing look. She was getting too good at those.

'How come you know Miss Morrison?'

'Oh, she's a client I did some work for.'

'Hmm,' said my daughter.

'Don't go jumping to conclusions. Wait a minute, how do you know her name?'

Ailsa grinned.

'Because she's my French teacher.' She stood on tiptoes and kissed me on the cheek. 'Got to go, Dad.'

She didn't look back as she headed off up the road, but she raised her right hand and fluttered her fingers.

'Enjoy your dinner on Saturday. I'll want details.'

There were times when she was so like her mum – or

rather the person her mum used to be – that she lifted my heart. Bumping into Dani had too, come to think of it.

That evening I flicked through all the news channels, looking for an update on Tavernier's death. There was no mention of it on any of them. There is only so much you can squeeze into a thirty-minute news cycle, and when you have to decide what is more important, the suspicious death of a senior judge or the marital problems of a pair of Hollywood airheads, I suppose some news editors would think it was a no-brainer.

So, I turned on my laptop.

I found more information on *The Telegraph* website. Tavernier had been beaten, but, interestingly, that wasn't what had killed him – although it can't have helped. The post-mortem revealed that he had suffered a fatal heart attack. The report said that he was the owner of the flat where he had been found, and that there had been several burglaries in the area. Apparently, the police were working on the theory that he had walked in on the thief, or thieves, while a robbery was in progress. They were continuing with their enquiries and had issued descriptions of the missing items – his wallet, his watch and his phone.

I sat back. The more I thought about Tavernier's death, the more certain I was that I had done the right thing in not getting Mary Pigott involved. It looked like a burglary that had gone wrong. And I knew exactly where Mary had been at the time Tavernier had died, because I had been watching her at her cottage – five hundred miles from the scene of the crime.

20

The next day I went into the office and wrote my account of the whole Mary Pigott investigation. I printed out a copy then deleted it from my laptop. I clipped the photo of Mary to the first page, then put the report in an envelope, thought for a moment, then wrote 'Carter' on it. Then I left the office carrying the envelope.

I went down one flight of stairs and stopped outside a solid wooden door with the words 'Thomas Szpac: Fine Tailoring, Repairs and Alterations' lettered on it. I knocked once and went in. A man aged about sixty was standing behind a counter. His name wasn't Thomas; it was Paul, though his second name was Szpac. Paul was carrying on the family business founded just after the Second World War by his dad.

Thomas had been one of the many Poles stationed in and around Dundee during the war. He had fought his way up through Italy – he'd given my granddad a hand sorting out the wee psychopath with the funny moustache, although I don't think they actually met one another.

Thomas had returned to Poland after the war, but quickly saw the way things were going. Poland had swapped one murdering psycho with a moustache for another, so Thomas returned to the only other place he knew well: Dundee.

Thomas passed away a few years back, but I heard his story from Paul when Eddie McLaren introduced us.

Eddie had refused to use any kind of computer and always wrote his reports on a typewriter. At first, he'd kept the reports in a steel filing cabinet, but then his office was broken into. It was just a couple of kids looking for cash, but it shook Eddie. He told me there was a lot of confidential information in his files, which could cause problems for clients if they fell into the wrong hands. He needed to store them somewhere more secure. And that somewhere was just one floor below him.

Eddie had been discussing the break-in with Thomas, who had recently taken over the premises on the floor below. The old tailor beckoned Eddie into a back room and showed him a plain wooden door. When he unlocked it, there wasn't a room or a cupboard behind it. Instead, Eddie found himself face to face with another door – only this one was made of steel and several inches thick.

Using another set of keys, Thomas unlocked the door in a complicated sequence, and then switched on a light to reveal a room. Eddie told me, 'It was huge! You could walk right in. And it was empty, bar a few box files on the floor.'

The safe had been installed over a hundred years ago, when the building was erected. When Thomas had taken over the office, he'd asked an old locksmith to check it over. The locksmith reported that there probably wasn't a safe-breaker alive who could open that lock. 'Mind you,' said the old guy, 'you might be able to blow it open, but the amount of explosives you'd need would bring the whole building down.'

'What do you think?' Thomas had asked Eddie.

'Worth a try,' had been Eddie's reply.

So, from that time on, Eddie had stored his files in the safe. And when I took over from Eddie, I saw no reason to change things.

As I entered his shop, clutching the Mary Pigott file, Paul said the same thing he always did: 'Another case successfully resolved, Allan?'

'Sort of,' I said.

A few moments later, I was in the safe. There were a few box files on the floor dating from Thomas's time but, ironically, Paul stored all his clients' details on a computer. As he said, 'I don't think that the waist measurements of my customers can be classed as being confidential, even at a stretch.'

Back in the day, Eddie had installed shelving and the files were logged in chronological order. I shelved the Mary Pigott file, then opened a card index and cross-referenced the file by name and date. Okay, I do know what century it is, but I could find exactly what I wanted in the time it took me to switch on a computer and start clicking on things. And I'd like to see a hacker hack his way through that door.

Paul locked up after me. I thanked him and returned to my office. I called Niddrie on his mobile. He answered on the third ring.

'Are we going into action? I'm still in a state of high alert.'

'Nothing so drastic,' I replied. 'I just wanted to ask if you still have that copy of Mary's photo.'

'I do.'

'Could you destroy it? There's no reason to keep it now.'

'Will do.' He rang off.

It was now late afternoon. I sat and looked at the phone for a while, but it didn't ring. I've found that not many people are looking for the services of a private investigator on a Friday afternoon. So, I closed the office and went home.

I decided to dine in, so I cut four thick slices off a crusty loaf and spread butter on two of them. Not too thick, certainly less than a quarter of an inch. Then I looked in the fridge and found some cold ham and slices of Jarlsberg cheese. I stacked the ham and cheese on the bread then added a layer of coarse grain mustard. Then I went back to the fridge where I knew a big bottle of Italian beer was lurking. I opened the bottle and took a mouthful. I wondered if I could interest a publisher in *The Private Detective's Cookbook*. It would be a thin volume, but an intriguing title.

Last Christmas, Ailsa had given me a holster, and I had attached it to my armchair. It wasn't for any kind of weapon, but the bottle of beer slotted perfectly into it.

With the beer in its proper place and a plate of sandwiches on my knee, I sat down and clicked on the TV. I was just in time to see a familiar face pop up on the local news. It was Nikki McKay and she was leaving Dundee Sheriff Court. It had been years since I'd last seen Nikki, and they hadn't been kind to her. She wasn't yet forty but, if I didn't know her, I'd have put her age at fifty at least.

A reporter appeared on screen and explained that Ms McKay had come home unexpectedly to find her teenage daughter, Shania, in bed with twenty-five-year-old Kevin McIntyre. That would have been a shock for any caring mother, but what made it worse was that Nikki was under the impression that she was engaged to the aforementioned Kevin.

When the police arrived, they found Shania locked in the bathroom, her mother battering on the door with a bloodstained frying pan. Kevin was on the bedroom floor in a dazed condition, naked and missing several teeth. The sheriff had taken into consideration that Nikki had acted under severe provocation; he fined her £100 and put her on probation for a year.

I have to say I was surprised. I didn't think that Nikki owned any kitchen utensils.

As the news report ended, the phone rang. I knew who it was.

'Hi, Bruce,' I said.

'Are you watching it?' Bruce replied. I could hear the glee in his voice.

'I am,' I said. 'Now, Bruce, I hope that you're not deriving pleasure from the misfortune of others.'

Bruce chuckled. 'Fuck that, I'm loving it.'

It was the only time I've ever heard Bruce swear.

21

My divorce from Hannah was pretty straightforward. She kept the house, which was only fair – after all, her dad had paid for it. There was no question of anyone paying anyone else maintenance, though George had pointed out to me that, as Hannah earned a lot more than I did, I could have made a case for her supporting me. I'm not sure if he was kidding or not. There was a formal agreement worked out regarding the custody of Ailsa but, in practice, Hannah was comfortable with me seeing her pretty much whenever I wanted.

The one thing I had insisted on was paying my share of the cost of Ailsa's upbringing – her school fees, holidays etc., although I was dreading the day she turned seventeen and came to me saying she'd seen a car she liked. She shared her mother's taste in cars – German and expensive. I knew I would have a hard job persuading her to consider Korean and cheap.

I knew some other guys who were divorced. They seemed to divide into two categories: half started chasing anyone with a pulse and wearing a skirt, and the rest sat at home moping. I am pleased to say I did neither.

I would meet up with George once a week for a few pints and I was a fairly regular attendee at office gatherings in the pub for people retiring or leaving. I tended to avoid stag parties; they could get really messy and there was no way I was going to spend three days in a drunken stupor in Eastern Europe, which was increasingly becoming the way to prepare for your forthcoming nuptials. As my dad once said, what's the difference between getting pissed in Prague and legless in Dundee? About three hundred quid and a sick bag on the flight home.

As for getting entangled with the fairer sex? Well, just a few weeks after my divorce, the assistant fashion editor on my paper made it obvious that she wouldn't say no if I asked her out. When I had first joined the paper, Jimmy Russell had called me over and said he was going to give me some advice. I sat down in front of his desk, waiting for the pearls of wisdom that would guide me on the path to becoming a proper newspaperman ... But all he had said was, 'Son, never shite in your own nest. Right, off you go.'

My nest has remained shite free ever since.

Through the office grapevine I managed to convey the message to the assistant fashion editor that, though I was flattered, I wasn't interested.

I did go out with a few girls, but never for long. I liked most of them and even slept with some of them, but there was never any chance of anything like a relationship developing. We had some fun and, when the time was right for both parties, we parted company amicably. No one got hurt.

When I became a private investigator, I made it a strict rule never to become involved with a client. To be honest, that hadn't been much of a problem. There was one woman who engaged me to look into a road accident she had been involved in. She was convinced she hadn't been at fault and wanted me to prove it. During our meetings she was extremely tactile and finally suggested that I come to her flat for a celebration drink when it was all over.

My enquiries did establish, without question, who was at fault in the accident. It was her; she'd been on her mobile phone when she ran into the back of another car. When I passed on the bad news, she stormed out of my office. So, no celebration drink, but I had insisted on a retainer up front before I took on the case.

But Dani wasn't a client. In fact, you could argue that she had never been a client. All I had done was suggest that she put up some posters. Okay, we were about to have dinner, but I was going to pay. So, it was with a completely clear conscience that I turned up at Vincenzo's bang on 8 p.m.

As I reached for the door handle, I heard footsteps behind me and I turned to see Dani.

'You're not going to knock me over again, I hope.' She smiled. She looked amazing in a long black coat over a white ruffled blouse and blue jeans.

'Not this time.' I smiled back.

The door opened and a young man with wavy black hair and a red waistcoat joined in the smiling. 'Miss Morrison! How good to see you again. Please, come this way.'

It was Saturday night, so the place was packed. The waiter led the way to our table. As we passed through the restaurant, I could see Dani being scrutinised. The men couldn't take their eyes off her face, while the women looked her up and down, checking out her make-up, hair and outfit. No one of either sex was giving me a second glance. I think I did a pretty good job of hiding my hurt feelings. For a moment my mind went back to over fifteen years ago when the door of The Ship opened and a different young woman had a similar effect. But that was a different life.

We were shown to a table for two at the back of the room. The waiter seated us and was about to hand out menus when a tall, slim man appeared at the table. He had thick black hair going grey at the temples and a gleaming set of white teeth. If you've ever seen a movie from the fifties featuring an Italian leading man, you'll get the idea.

'No menus, Gino,' he said to the waiter. 'I'll take care of Miss Morrison personally.'

The waiter took Dani's coat and retreated. The newcomer leaned forward and kissed Dani's hand. He made no attempt to kiss mine.

'What d'you recommend this evening, Vincenzo?' asked Dani.

Vincenzo broke into a torrent of Italian. Dani listened carefully and asked a couple of questions. My knowledge of the language extends to two words – *Peroni* and *Moretti* – so I thought it best to let them get on with it.

Dani held up a hand and Vincenzo stopped in mid-flow. She turned to me. 'I'm sorry, Allan. I'm being so rude, but I normally go with what Vincenzo suggests. Is there anything that you don't like to eat?'

'Not too keen on Brussels sprouts,' I said.

Vincenzo looked offended.

'There's no place for that vegetable in my kitchen,' he said.

He and Dani resumed their conversation. After another minute, he beamed at her and swept off to the kitchen.

Dani put her hand on mine.

'I hope you don't mind, but I've ordered for both of us. You did say you liked Italian food. Believe me, you'll love it.'

'I'm sure I will. But what about something to drink? I'll get the wine list.'

Dani squeezed my hand.

'No need. I told Vincenzo that we'd have a bottle of the house red. It's very good quality.' A look of concern passed across her face. 'Oh, I didn't think. You do drink wine, don't you?'

I thought of making some kind of smart reply involving squirrels and trees, but I decided that wouldn't be appropriate so simply said, 'I enjoy a glass of wine.'

Dani laughed and squeezed my hand again.

'That's perfect!'

She was right. It was perfect.

Before the starter arrived I said, 'You speak Italian?'

'I lived there for a while. When I come here, it's a chance to practise.'

'But you teach French,' I said.

Dani looked puzzled for a moment, then her face brightened. 'Of course. Linton . . . your daughter's Ailsa.'

Linton was the name on Ailsa's birth certificate. Hannah had never changed it.

'She spotted us the other day,' I said.

Dani raised an eyebrow, so I gave her the answer to the question before she asked it.

'I was married to her mother. We divorced nearly ten years ago.'

At that moment, Vincenzo reappeared with a large carafe. He looked at me. 'Would you like to try the wine, sir?'

'Oh, stop it, Vincenzo,' Dani broke in. 'You know we'll love it. Go ahead and pour.'

'As you say, Miss Morrison.'

He poured a generous amount into our glasses. I was about to sample the wine when Dani picked up her glass and glugged down a fair mouthful. So I did the same.

'Well?' she said.

I looked up at Vincenzo, who raised an eyebrow.

'It's excellent,' I said.

'Of course it is,' he said. He placed the carafe on the table and left.

'You could have spent three times as much on a bottle from the wine list, but it wouldn't taste any better than this. Vincenzo advised me to order it when I first came here.'

'He likes you, doesn't he?'

Dani grinned at me. 'Yes, he does, but don't get the wrong idea. His wife, Claudia, is cooking our meal and Gino is one of his three sons who work here. Vincenzo likes people who love good food and wine. I qualify on both counts!'

'So,' I said. 'You teach my daughter French.'

'Yes, I do. But I'm bound by teacher/pupil confidentiality. I can't tell you how she's doing.' She saw the look on my face then burst into laughter. 'I'm teasing! Seriously, though, she's a pleasure to teach. She's clever, but she also works hard. You must be very proud of her.'

'I am, but I suspect she gets her brains from her mother.'

'She has a great sense of fun. I think she might get that from you, Allan.'

Before I could think of a reply, I was saved by the arrival of the starter. It consisted mainly of tomato and mozzarella cheese, but there were other things in there that I didn't recognise. It was delicious.

As the plates were cleared away, I said, 'You aren't a native of my fair city, are you?'

Dani gave me a mock-rueful grin. 'Ah, I forgot. You are a detective, Allan. What gave me away?'

'I thought I detected the trace of an accent when you first

came into my office. You teach French, but I don't think you come from France.'

'You're correct. I come from further east.'

If she wanted me to know how much further east, she would tell me in her own time, so I said, 'How did you come to be teaching French in Dundee?'

She shrugged and said, 'It's a long story. Just let me say that before I came to Scotland I taught at schools in England. But, for one reason or another, I never felt settled. Then I saw an ad for the school here. I applied and, to my good fortune, I was given the job. I like it here. The staff are friendly and the pupils, with few exceptions, are bright and willing to learn. It makes my job so much more enjoyable. And Dundee isn't a bad place to live.'

Dundee hasn't had the best of reputations over the years. In fact, a judge once described it as 'a sink of atrocity' thanks to the nefarious activities and other antisocial behaviour of its citizens. But that was when the harbour was full of whaling ships, and I think it's safe to say the city has improved its image since then. Nevertheless, it was good to hear an outsider speak positively about the old place.

Another waiter appeared at our table. He was short and plump and he beamed at Dani as he placed plates of spaghetti in front of us.

'Enjoy, Miss Morrison,' he said.

'Thank you, Francisco.' Dani paused and looked at me before digging her fork into the food. 'Another of Vincenzo's sons,' she said. 'Takes after his mother.'

The spaghetti was laced with clams, prawns and a kick of chilli. It was a delight, but it wasn't the biggest plate of pasta I'd ever eaten. Dani read my mind.

'Don't worry, the main course has still to come.'

We talked as we ate. I told her about my schooldays, my time at the newspaper and how I became an investigator. She laughed at the stories of the criminals and clients – sometimes one and the same – that I had encountered on the way.

Dani had funny stories of her own to tell – mainly about pupils and parents. I noted that they all dated back to the time she arrived in Dundee. Nothing before then.

The main course arrived: steak and chips. But I had never had steak and chips like it. The beef was rare and covered in a rich sauce – tomatoes, capers and a handful of black olives thrown in for good measure. The chips were thin and crisp and dusted with some kind of spice.

We tend to think of steak and chips as the quintessential British dish. And if you like plain, uncomplicated food, our version is hard to beat. But I've eaten steak all over Europe and, with the exception of France, where they seem to refuse to actually cook the meat, I've loved it every time. Vincenzo's was up there with the very best.

I washed down the final mouthful with the last drop of wine and sat back, reflecting that I hadn't felt so full since I got carried away and attempted a third Dundee pie. Dani looked at my empty plate.

'I chose well then?' she said.

'Oh, yes,' I said, wondering if I could get away with loosening my belt buckle.

'Good.' She beamed. 'Now for dessert.'

I shook my head. 'I'd love to, but I just couldn't.'

'Nonsense. Tell you what, we'll share.'

She caught Vincenzo's eye and held up one finger. He smiled, nodded and disappeared into the kitchen. Moments later, he came back with a plate and two spoons.

Dani grinned. 'Panna cotta! My favourite!'

So, we shared dessert. By that I mean I managed a couple of spoonfuls and Dani devoured the rest. She sat back and I swear she licked her lips. I shook my head. Where did she put it all?

Again, she seemed to read my mind. 'I'm just one of those lucky people who can eat what they want and never put on a milligram,' she said with a shrug.

Vincenzo came over, carrying two small brandy glasses. He looked at me. 'You enjoyed, sir?'

'Very much. The sauce with the steak was outstanding. An old family recipe?'

'Not quite. Claudia makes it up as she goes along. It's never the same two nights running.'

He laid the brandy in front of us.

'Compliments of the house. Italian brandy ... *Vecchia Romagna*. It will aid the digestion.'

As we sipped the spirit, I looked round the restaurant. We were the only ones left. My granddad used to say that good company turned the hours into minutes. He could talk a load of old rubbish at times, but he'd got that one right.

I drained the glass and got to my feet.

'I'll just go and settle up.'

Dani put her hand on my arm. 'No, let me pay half.'

'I asked you out, I pay the bill.'

Dani stood up. 'I must go to the bathroom. I'll see you at the counter.'

I went to the counter, where Vincenzo had my bill waiting. Even after I added a decent tip it was ridiculously reasonable.

Looking serious, Vincenzo said, 'Miss Morrison sometimes eats here with friends and twice she has come here with gentlemen. She has never brought either gentleman back again.'

Before I could say anything, Dani reappeared and Gino helped her on with her coat. Vincenzo held open the door.

He gave me the briefest of smiles as I stepped out. 'Thank you, sir. I hope to see you again.'

The door of the restaurant closed, leaving us on the pavement. Dani smiled at me.

'Thank you for a wonderful evening,' she said.

I looked at my watch. It was well after midnight. 'Look,' I said, 'I know you didn't want me to pick you up, but you must let me take you home. You can't walk around on your own at this time of night.'

Dani thought for a moment then said, 'Of course. It's not far, about a ten-minute walk.'

As we walked I thought about what Vincenzo had said.

'We private investigators are a suspicious lot, so I can't help thinking that was a bit of a test.'

'What do you mean?'

'Hmm, I got the impression that one of the reasons we went there tonight was so that you could let Vincenzo run the rule over me.'

Dani feigned surprise. 'And do you think you passed the test?'

'I don't know. What do you think?'

Dani walked on in front of me. 'Let's just say I've never known Vincenzo to offer anyone a free brandy before.'

We reached a crossroads known as the Sinderins. It's a corruption of the word 'sundering', the splitting of the ways. Blackness Avenue branches off to the right.

Dani stopped at the entrance to a block of flats and turned to me.

'I think I'll be safe from here. My apartment is on the third floor.'

She looked seriously at me.

'I'm not going to invite you in, Allan. We barely know one another and I'd prefer to take things slowly. That is, if you do want to see me again.'

Squirrels and woods flitted briefly through my mind.

'I'd like that very much,' I replied. 'I'll call you.'

Five minutes later, I was hailing a taxi on the Perth Road. I reckoned I'd just had one of the best nights of my life.

22

Next morning I rose early, which for me on a Sunday meant I was showered and dressed before 11 a.m. I switched on my record deck and started to sift through my album collection. I'd heard that vinyl was making a comeback. In the Linton family it had never gone away. I had nearly all my dad's stuff from the sixties, plus some LPs I'd picked up from a great second-hand record shop in Dundee.

I had just settled on the Searchers' first album when my mobile phone rang. It was Ailsa. I was a bit surprised. I thought she would have called before 7 a.m.

'Hi, Dad. I had a sleepover at Kirstie's.'

Kirstie was one of my daughter's school friends. Her family lived in one of the big stone houses in the Ferry.

'I was just wondering if you fancied going for breakfast. I could be there in a little while. You are in your flat, aren't you?'

I walked over to the front door and opened it. Ailsa had her phone to her ear and an overnight bag at her feet. She gave me a big grin. My daughter doesn't do embarrassed.

'Hi, Dad.'

'Come in,' I said. 'I'll just get my coat and my wallet.'

Ailsa sauntered into the flat. I switched off the record

deck, got my jacket from the hall cupboard and turned to find her peeking into my bedroom.

'Save yourself the trouble. There's no one here.'

Ailsa nodded and headed to the door. 'Let's go and eat. I'm starving. Kirstie's mum doesn't do proper breakfasts.' She made a face. 'Whole grain cereal and soya milk. Yeuch!'

Ailsa might like to sit in trendy coffee shops and be admired, but when it comes to Sunday breakfasts she is a traditionalist. There's a place in the Ferry that does a proper fry-up. You can feel your arteries clog up as you eat. Five minutes later, we were seated there and the waitress came to take our order.

'What would you like, miss?' she asked.

She was obviously new.

Ailsa had her fork in one hand and her knife in the other, sharp ends pointing upwards.

'Everything.'

The waitress seemed to reel back before she recovered her composure and turned to me.

'And you, sir?'

I was still feeling the effects of my Italian extravaganza, so I asked for some scrambled eggs on toast and a pot of tea for two.

Ailsa tilted her head to one side, leaned forward and gave me a sly grin.

'Well, Dad, how'd it go?'

'The food was excellent. We talked and I had fun. I think Miss Morrison did too. At the end of the evening I walked her to her door then caught a taxi home. I was tucked up in bed before one.'

Ailsa sat back in her chair. She looked at me in disbelief. 'Is that it?'

'You wanted details.' I smiled. 'You got them.'

'Jeez, Dad. What are you? Fifteen?'

'No, if I was fifteen my hormones would've been raging and I'd probably have behaved inappropriately. I'm a mature, sensible adult and I know how to conduct myself when taking out someone like Dani.'

Ailsa grinned and punched me on the arm, thankfully remembering to put down her knife first.

'You like her, don't you?'

I was saved by the arrival of our breakfasts. Ailsa's plate was piled high with fried egg, black pudding, sausage, bacon, fried bread, mushrooms and beans. Her eyes lit up. For the second time in less than twenty-four hours I was sitting opposite a female who seemed to be able to eat anything she wanted without putting on an ounce. Maybe I should challenge her to a pie-eating contest. I'd probably lose.

There wasn't much talking done over the next twenty-five minutes. Finally, Ailsa leaned back in her chair and burped.

'That was great, Dad. Thanks. Now, where was I?'

I held up my hand. 'You asked for details. You got them.'

'Okay. I'd better call Mum. She said she'd pick me up.'

While I paid the bill, Ailsa phoned Hannah.

'Mum says she'll be here in about twenty minutes,' she told me when she'd hung up.

'It's a nice day. Let's take a walk till she gets here,' I said.

We strolled round to the old harbour. It was sunny, without a breath of wind, and the Tay lay perfectly still. I looked across the harbour to the castle. It dates from the fifteenth century and, yes, it had also received a bit of a kicking from the English, although, to be fair, various Scottish factions had fought over it too. The story I liked best, though, concerned the time in 1855 when the War Office acquired the castle to defend the harbour against the Russians. That was during the Crimean War and my guess was that the mandarins in Whitehall had got it into their heads that the fiendish Russkies were planning to deliver a knock-out blow to the British war effort by capturing Dundee. But I reckon word had reached St Petersburg about the 'sink of atrocity', because the Tsar and his boys decided to stay well clear.

I knew that Ailsa wasn't finished with her interrogation, so I got in first. 'How's Janette?'

'Gran? Oh, she's fine. She always asks how you are after I've seen you.'

I'd always liked my ex-mother-in-law and regretted breaking my promise to her that I would look after Hannah. We spoke on the phone occasionally and had bumped into each other in town a few times. Once we had gone for coffee and I'd mentioned that broken promise, but Janette had laid her hand on my arm and told me that she didn't blame me.

'Fergus should never have interfered,' she'd said fiercely. 'And Hannah shouldn't have let him.'

Then her expression softened. 'You know, Fergus wasn't always the way he is now. When we first met he was kind and considerate . . . and full of fun. That's why I fell in love with him.'

She saw the look of disbelief on my face and laughed. 'I know, hard to believe, isn't it? I know what you're thinking. What happened? Well, when he was a young lawyer, the senior partner took him aside and told him that if he really wanted to succeed, he had to toughen up, become more ruthless. Well, it worked. He went on to start his own law firm.' Her lips twisted. 'And took a lot of clients from his old firm with him.'

She shook her head sadly.

'I hate to say it, but I think Hannah has taken after her father. She was a fool, Allan. I don't think she realised how lucky she was having you.'

Then her face brightened and she added, 'However, thanks to you, I have my wonderful granddaughter.'

How many guys have had their mother-in-law say nice things like that about them?

I looked down at my daughter. She took after her mother in so many ways. I hoped that Dani was right that she got her sense of fun from me, and that that would never change.

'Mum said she'd pick me up at the cafe, so maybe we'd better head back that way,' Ailsa said. 'So, are you going to see Miss Morrison again?'

I knew I shouldn't have encouraged Ailsa to look up the Spanish Inquisition. She was relentless.

'I hope so,' I replied. 'I've got to call her.'

'Don't leave it too long, Dad. Miss Morrison's really cool. Plus, I've got a French test coming up. If you treat her right, I might get an A.'

Ailsa smiled at me. 'Seriously, though, Dad, I hope it works out for you. I really like Miss Morrison.' Then she laughed. 'Besides, you're not getting any younger!'

We had almost reached the cafe. The black Merc was sitting outside.

Ailsa turned to me and said quietly, 'I haven't told mum about Miss Morrison and, in case you're wondering, and I'm sure you're not, Mum isn't seeing anyone.'

As Ailsa put her bag in the boot, Hannah rolled down her window.

'The usual healthy breakfast, I take it?' she said.

163

'Look it this way, just be grateful our daughter has no issues with body image.'

Hannah smiled sweetly. 'Did you enjoy your meal at Vincenzo's? Good food there, isn't it?'

Ailsa looked at me over the roof of the car. She shrugged, opened her eyes wide and shook her head. She had said she hadn't told her mother and I believed her. I suspected Hannah had received a phone call this morning from one of her friends. Dundee is a small place.

Ailsa got into the car and called out, 'See you again soon, Dad. Love you!'

Hannah rolled up her window and the Coupé moved smoothly away.

I walked back to my flat and minutes later the Searchers were belting out 'Love Potion Number 9'. It's a song about a guy who can't get a girlfriend.

23

The next morning I didn't get into the office till 10 a.m. There was an email waiting for me from the director of the pub chain – the one who had hired me to find out where all their profits had been going. They were having the same problem in their place in Arbroath. He wanted me to go in undercover again.

I thought about it. Arbroath was only a thirty-minute drive away and the pub boss had paid me well. I emailed him back to say that I was interested and that he should send me more details. Then there was a knock at the door and, before I could say anything, two men entered.

One was of medium height and slightly overweight, wearing jeans and a leather blouson over a white shirt open at the neck. His curly brown hair would need a cut in the next couple of days. I'd guess that he was in his early thirties.

The other was the same height and age, but pencil thin. He, too, was wearing a leather coat but his came to mid-calf. Under a beautifully fitted suit he wore a blue shirt with a white collar and cuffs and a tightly-knotted striped tie. He didn't get his hair cut; he got it *styled*. He looked like a public relations man or an advertising executive. His companion looked like the taxi driver who had brought him here.

So, I was slightly taken aback when the taxi driver stepped forward, smiled and held out his hand.

'Allan Linton? Hi, I'm Phil Nash. Good to meet you.'

I took his hand and shook it. His grip was dry and firm.

His accent was English; he sounded like he could be from anywhere within a twenty-mile radius of London.

The PR guy had taken up station to one side of the door. I don't know what his accent was. That's because he didn't say anything. He just looked around the room.

I indicated the chair in front of my desk. 'Please sit. What can I do for you, Mr Nash?'

'Call me Phil. Look, Allan, I'll come straight to the point. A friend of mine told me he came to see you a couple of weeks ago. He was doing me a favour.'

'Your friend's name?'

Nash paused for a moment and looked at me closely before answering, 'Tavernier. Bernard Tavernier.'

So, Tavernier's mysterious client did exist.

'A man did come here, but he called himself Carter,' I replied. 'I only discovered what his real name was after he was found dead. Perhaps you can explain why he lied to me and why a senior judge was doing you a favour.'

Nash pursed his lips. He looked up at the ceiling then back down at me. 'He didn't lie. Not as such. I'd asked him to be discreet, so maybe that's why he thought it best not to give his real name.'

I made no comment, so Nash went on, 'I needed to find someone – a girl called Tina Lamont who, I think, comes from here. Bernie was an old friend who knew people in Dundee. He offered to use his connections to try to find Tina. One of them must have recommended you.'

I took a deep breath then said, 'Tavernier never told me why he wanted to find Miss Lamont. Maybe you can.'

For a moment, Nash seemed embarrassed, but then he looked me directly in the eye and said, 'It wasn't just Tina I wanted to find. I also wanted to see my kid.' He shook his head. 'I met Tina when she lived in London. We began seeing one another. The trouble was, I was engaged to someone else. I was a bloody idiot. Then Tina got pregnant. Before she had the baby, she asked what I was going to do about it. What could I do? My wedding was all planned. My head was a mess.

'Tina disappeared and I've not heard from her since. I don't blame her. I acted like a complete dickhead.'

'So why are you so keen to find her now?'

Nash leaned forward and clasped his hands on his knees. 'My fiancée found out and went mental. The wedding was called off and it won't be back on again. She isn't the forgiving kind.'

I looked up at the other guy. I was beginning to think that he wasn't in PR, because if he was, he wasn't helping his client present a very good image.

'Look,' Nash said, 'I don't want to cause Tina any problems. What we had was never going to last. But I want to do right by my kid. I don't even know if it's a boy or a girl. I know I live five hundred miles away, but maybe I could see the kid from time to time. And I want to help out with money and stuff. I gave Bernie the cash to hire you. So, in effect, I'm your client. I have to ask you. Did you find Tina?'

I thought for a moment. Mary had said that her child's father had wanted nothing to do with her after she became pregnant, so what Nash had said rang true. He could have had a change of heart but, if I asked him why, he would know that I had found her. I wasn't ready to share that yet.

So, I said, 'No, I never found anyone called Tina Lamont.'

That was true. I had found someone called Mary Pigott, not Tina Lamont.

Nash looked disappointed. The guy at the door looked bored.

Then Nash looked straight at me. 'I authorised Bernie to pay another five grand if you found Tina. That offer still stands.'

'I'm sorry, but, as I said, I was unable to find Miss Lamont. I don't think there's any more I can do.'

'Still, if any new information turns up, I'd appreciate it if you contacted me. Do you have a pen and paper?'

I handed him a pen and a writing pad and Nash scribbled down a mobile number.

'You can contact me on this number.' He handed the pad back to me. 'Well, we had better be off. We've got a long drive in front of us.'

'One last thing,' I said. 'Have you heard anything more about Tavernier's death?'

Nash grimaced. 'Not a thing, I'm afraid. Awful what happened. The police think he interrupted some burglars. Happens even in the best parts of London. I hope they catch the bastards.'

Nash shook my hand and left, followed by the other guy, who paused in the doorway and looked me in the eye for the first time. It reminded me of a photo I'd once seen of a fox caught in headlights and looking straight at the camera. There was the same baleful look in his eyes. Forget the animated films and the children's books. I've seen the aftermath of a fox's visit to a hen coop. They are not cute and cuddly. The man turned and followed Nash down the stairs.

I thought I'd made a good decision in not telling them about Mary.

I went to the window overlooking the street. A few seconds later, I watched as Nash and his companion exited the building. They crossed the street and got into a Range Rover with darkened windows. I waited ten minutes, but they didn't seem in any hurry to start their long drive.

I left it another fifteen minutes then took another look. The Range Rover hadn't moved. I called Niddrie. He answered on the third ring.

'Where are you?' I asked.

'I'm in TK Maxx. Even private detectives need new underwear from time to time. But don't worry, I'm still on high alert.'

'There are a couple of English guys sitting in a Range Rover outside the office. I need to go and see Mary Pigott and I'm pretty sure they're going to follow me. I don't want that to happen.'

'Go and wait in the entrance to your building. Don't let them see you. Give me ten minutes then get to your car.'

He rang off and I went down to the entrance. I looked across at the Range Rover. I couldn't see who was inside, but I was sure Nash and the other guy were still there. On the pavement beside the Range Rover was a row of dark-grey bins.

A few minutes later, a refuse truck pulled up behind the Range Rover. Then a second truck appeared and parked diagonally in front of Nash's car, completely blocking it in. My phone rang. It was Niddrie.

'Go now.'

I sprinted out of the entrance and, as I dodged into the alley leading to where I parked my car, I could hear Nash arguing with the cleansing operatives, or 'bin men', as they are better known in Dundee.

'Get that fucking truck out of my way,' Nash said.

'No need to be like that, pal. Just doing our job.'

A fellow cleansing operative joined in, adding, 'Aye, you shouldn't be parked here anyway.'

I got to my Hyundai, started her up and drove out of the alley. As I turned onto the main street, I saw that the argument was still going on. The cleansing operatives had stopped work altogether. Nash was red in the face, but they were all big guys and nobody was telling them what to do.

A hundred yards up the road I passed Niddrie standing on the pavement. He looked at me and his cheeks twitched.

I waited till I was on the dual carriageway to Forfar before I called him. I'd already checked my mirror three times and there was no sign of pursuit.

'How'd you do that?' I asked.

'I told the bin men that the guys in the Range Rover were debt collectors from England sent here to track down people who still hadn't paid their poll tax and my mate was trying to get away from them.'

'They believed that?'

'I noticed the SNP stickers on the trucks. I think that telling them the guys in the Rover were English was what swung it. Anyway, who were they?'

'It's a long story. I'll explain when I get back.'

As I drove, I hoped that Mary was still at her cottage. I couldn't have called ahead because I didn't have a number for her. Anyway, this was one conversation I wanted to have face to face.

Half an hour later, I pulled up in front of Mary's cottage. As I walked up to the door, it opened. Mary stood there and I could see she wasn't pleased.

'What the hell are you doing here?' she hissed. 'You promised me you wouldn't bother me again.'

'No, I said that I wouldn't tell anyone where you were, and I've kept that promise. But something's happened and we have to talk.'

Mary turned and led the way into the sitting room.

'Keep your voice down. I've just got wee Colin to sleep.'

We sat facing each other.

'Just over an hour ago, a man walked into my office and said that he'd asked Bernard Tavernier to help him find Tina Lamont.'

I could almost hear Mary's teeth gritting.

'I told you,' she said, 'I don't know any Tina Lamont or Bernard Tavernier – or anyone he was helping.'

'Here's the thing. This guy said he was the father of Tina's child. And he wanted to help.'

Mary's eyes widened – not much, but just enough for me to notice.

I went on, 'He was English, and he said his name was Phil Nash.'

'I don't know any Phil Nash,' said Mary quickly.

'The last Englishman to come and see me lied about his name. I've a feeling Mr Nash isn't being entirely truthful either. I'd say he was in his thirties, curly brown hair, could lose a few pounds . . .'

Mary took a deep breath.

I went on, 'He had this guy with him. Didn't get a name for him. Slim, really smart dresser. But eyes like a corpse –'

Mary moaned. She started to get to her feet, but then slumped back into her chair and looked pleadingly at me.

'You didn't tell them you found me. Oh, please tell me you didn't.'

'I told you, I haven't told anyone. But I think that it's time you told me the truth, Mary. For a start, is he the father of your son?'

Mary laughed bitterly. 'God no.' Her expression turned panicked. 'Wait. You said he came to see you. What if he's followed you here?'

'You don't have to worry about that. I made sure he couldn't follow me. Mary, I'll help you if I can. But I need to know everything.'

Mary sighed.

'All I ever wanted to do was dance,' she began. 'That's all that mattered to me, which meant I wasn't exactly interested in studying. So, I left school with just a few passes at E and D level. But, hey, I'd been the star performer in the school productions of musicals.

'After school, I joined a couple of the local musical societies and people kept telling me how talented I was. I'd moved from one crappy job to another, so it seemed that the obvious thing to do was become a professional dancer. Which meant I had to go to London.

'That wasn't a problem for me. The problem was that London was full of girls from all over the country who'd been told they were talented. The competition was brutal. I got one job, but the show closed after a week and I didn't even get paid. I tried to get a job teaching dance in schools but there were thirty girls going after the same position.

'So, I ended up waitressing, which was worse than the jobs I'd had back home. I was sharing a flat with some other girls, but I could barely pay my share of the rent.'

Then Mary paused. I wondered whether things were about to get dark. I was right.

'One of the girls in the flat had this friend who used to come and visit her,' Mary continued. 'Her name was Candy.'

I looked at Mary.

'Yeah, I know,' she said. 'Probably not the name on her birth certificate. Anyway, one day Candy said that her friend had told her I was a dancer. She said that if I was looking for work, maybe she could help. The place she worked at was on the lookout for new dancers, and the money was a lot better than a waitress got paid.'

'I take it Candy wasn't starring in the latest West End smash hit,' I said.

'No, it was a lap dancing club.'

Mary looked up at me defiantly, but I said, 'I'm not here to judge you, Mary.'

'I knew what it was, but I was sick of serving plates of chips in a shitty cafe to morons who couldn't keep their hands to themselves. So, I went with Candy to this club. Let's face it, most of the dancers you see on TV these days are practically naked. Most of the girl bands too, come to that. On the way, Candy told me none of the girls used their real names and it would be best if I didn't either.'

'So that's when you became Tina Lamont?'

Mary nodded and smiled. 'Yeah, we were passing a nail bar called Tina's and there was a bakery next door.

Lamont's Cakes and Pastries. Tina Lamont, the perfect name for a lap dancer.

'Anyway, Candy introduced me to the club owner. His name was Bobby Kagan. You met him this morning.'

'The one who called himself Phil Nash?' I said.

'That's him.'

I thought, what is it with the English? They come up here and burn down our church, besiege our castle and don't even have the decency to tell us their real names.

'The guy with him is Oliver. If he has a second name, I never heard it. He's Bobby's driver, fixer, bodyguard – whatever Bobby needs.' She shivered. 'One of his jobs was to keep the girls in line. He seemed to enjoy that. He doesn't like women.

'Anyway, I did an audition for Bobby, which meant I took off my clothes and gyrated around a bit. He liked what he saw, and I started that night. Candy told me the trick was to just listen to the music and cut yourself off. The reality was that the club's clientele wasn't all that different from the morons in the cafe, only they had more cash to spend. After a while, I started to forget they were there.

'I was earning more money than I had in the cafe, but not all that much. Bobby didn't actually pay the dancers. We just got the tips from the punters, but Bobby even took a cut of that. Some of the girls complained, but they were told to speak to Oliver, so they just shut up. One girl kept going on about it, so Oliver took her out of the club. We never saw her again.'

Mary hesitated then said, 'Candy told me that there was a way of making big money.'

'Don't tell me,' I said. 'You had to be extra nice to customers.'

'Yeah. Some of the girls did. Bobby didn't mind as long as they didn't do anything in the club. Candy tried to persuade me, but I told her I didn't want to get involved. Okay, I was dancing naked in front of men, but I wasn't prepared to go further. Believe it or not, there's a difference.

'The girls who were doing extras usually had a drug problem. That included Candy. Guess what? She began to use more and more, and it started to show. In the end, Bobby threw her out of the club. He said that his customers weren't paying to see some ratbag with needle tracks in her arms. I heard she ended up on the streets, but I never saw her again.'

Mary paused. It was clear that this was taking a toll on her.

'Want a break?' I said. 'Can I get you some water?'

She nodded. 'There's a bottle in the fridge.'

I walked through to the tiny kitchen. On the way I passed a small bedroom containing a cot. I looked in. The wee lad was still fast asleep. It's a shitty world and parents should protect their children from as much of it as they can.

The kitchen was immaculate. No dishes in the sink. Everything was neatly tidied away and the work surfaces were spotless. Mary had turned her life around.

I found the water and took it back to her. She had a sip, then took a deep breath and went on, 'I'd been there about a year and it was the week before Christmas. It was a busy time. Lots of office parties coming in. Mainly men but there were some women too. Why would they want to do that?' She shook her head like she couldn't believe it.

'Anyway, one night this lot of lawyers came in. They were all from some big practice. Bobby loved lawyers. He said they got rat-arsed quickly and didn't realise the stuff they were drinking wasn't real champagne, but some camel's piss he was buying by the tankerful and charging a fortune for.

'This group of lawyers were all pretty young, but there was this one older guy – in his sixties. I don't think he'd ever been in a place like that before. Some of the younger ones bought a dance for him and they picked me. Normally, I never looked at their faces, but I took a peek at the expression on this old boy's face. I remember thinking, he's never seen a woman naked before.

'A couple of nights later, he came back. This time he was alone and sober. He wanted me to dance for him. After that he'd come into the club every two or three weeks. He always insisted on me dancing. Even when I was with someone else, he'd wait till I was finished.'

'So that's how you came to meet Bernard Tavernier,' I said. 'Didn't you find this a bit creepy?'

'Some of the punters think they can touch you up. More than once I saw guys playing with themselves. Bobby's bouncers always put a stop to that. I don't think he cared about the girls, but there was something about the conditions of his license. But Bernard never did any of that stuff. He was harmless. He just sat there and watched me. And he always tipped me well – really well.

'It was usually about three in the morning before I finished work. One night I came out of the club and he was waiting for me. He asked if he could give me a lift home. Well, I wish I had a pound for every time I heard that one. But he promised me there wouldn't be any funny business and, like I said, he seemed harmless. And he did exactly what he said he would. He took me straight to the flat. He even got out and opened the door for me.

'This went on every time he came to the club. He never

even attempted to give me a kiss on the cheek. Then one night he said he wanted to show me something. He drove me to this block of flats. It looked really expensive. I found out later that flats there went for a million plus. A bit different from the place I was staying in. Anyway, he opened the door as usual, but I didn't get out. He said I wasn't to be concerned. That's what he said; I wasn't to be concerned. He looked so serious and, to be honest, I was starting to trust him. So, I followed him to this flat.

'It was amazing. I'd never been in any place like it. Beautiful furniture. The kitchen had everything, only it looked like no one ever used it. He explained that he lived in a village outside London, but he used this place during the week when he was working in the city. At that time, I thought he was just a lawyer. I didn't find out he was a judge till later.

'He said I was welcome to stay there. I would have my own bedroom and I wouldn't have to pay rent. I asked him what he expected in return and he said nothing, absolutely nothing. I said I'd have to think about it and he gave me a number to call him. I went back to the flat I was sharing and looked around. The place was a tip and it stank. So I called the number and Bernard told me to meet him at his flat that evening. I packed a bag and moved in.'

Mary sat back and closed her eyes.

'Bernard used to come in every Monday night and leave on Friday morning. He spent the weekends with his wife. I looked him up on the Internet and I found that they didn't have family. I think she came from money. I also found out that he wasn't just a lawyer. He was a judge. I didn't have to pay any bills and he made sure the fridge was always full. I started to put money away. I knew it was never going to last, but I hoped to save enough to make a fresh start somewhere. Lap dancing isn't exactly a long-term career.'

Mary opened her eyes and sat up.

'You know, I never met another soul the whole time I lived there. A bloody great block of flats and I never saw anyone going in or coming out of any of the other flats. That's London, I suppose.'

So that was why there was no report of anyone seeing a girl living in the flat when I saw the news of Tavernier's death.

'Bernard stopped coming to the club,' Mary continued. 'He said that he'd been lucky so far, but it was only a matter of time before someone recognised him. So, one night he sat me down and said he had something to ask me. He said I could say no and he'd understand completely, but I knew what he was going to say. He was practically squirming with embarrassment, so I made it easy for him. I told him that if he wanted me to dance for him, I would. There was one more little thing, too, but again I didn't have to do it.

'He wanted me to dress up first. He started to say no, no, he shouldn't have asked, but I gave him a peck on the cheek and said it would be okay.'

Mary gave me a sad smile.

'What else could I do? The poor old bugger was so grateful. So, he brought all those costumes and uniforms to the flat . . . policewoman, nurse, secretary and a naughty schoolgirl. Some of the time I think I was meant to be famous women from history. He told me the names, but I didn't have a clue who he was talking about. I told you, I didn't study too hard at school. He'd just sit there while I took them off and gave him his own private lap dance. I had only one rule. No photographs.'

'But he had that photo of you,' I said.

'I know. He must've taken it on his phone when I wasn't looking.'

'I said I wouldn't judge you, and I'm not,' I said. 'But didn't you think this was all a bit, well, weird?'

Mary sighed. 'It might be weird in your world, Mr Linton, but down there it can pass as normal. And, like I said, Bernard never tried anything. It was too good to last of course. One night I went to the club and Bobby called me into his office. He had this smirk on his face. "Well, well," he said. "Little Miss Goody Two Shoes is shagging some old guy. Who would've believed it?"

'He said he'd spotted me getting into Bernard's car. He'd recognised Bernard, so he'd had Oliver follow me back to the flat.

'"So," he said. "Shacked up with a judge. Very cosy. That could be useful to me." I asked him what he meant by that and he said he could sell the story to the papers. He didn't know what the going rate for exposing a kinky judge was, but it might be worth a few grand. But he wasn't going to do that. Instead, this could be the gift that kept on giving. I didn't say anything, so he went on, saying things like what if some guy had been a naughty boy? What if he ended up in court? What if the judge in the trial was Bernard Tavernier? He could go to the accused and tell him he might have some influence with the judge. And, for a fee of course, he could use that influence to get the naughty boy a lighter sentence. Maybe, in the right circumstances, make sure that he got off altogether.

'He wanted me to help him install a camera in the flat so that he could film us having sex. I said it wasn't like that. I just lived there. "Oh, yeah?" he said. "Lap dancer and senior judge share a flat but are just good friends. Think I was born yesterday?"

'I didn't tell him about Bernard's little "requests". That would have been even worse, I suppose. I told him that I wouldn't do it. That's when he hit me. Then he asked me if I knew that Oliver was becoming interested in science, in particular the effects of acid on human skin. He'd already carried out a few experiments.'

Mary took another sip of water. Her hand shook.

'Bobby said it'd take a couple of weeks to organise. He had to get the audio and video equipment and a couple of guys to install it all. All I had to do was let them into the flat when Bernard wasn't there.

'But there was another problem. I found out that I was pregnant. And worse, one of the other girls found out too. She caught me being sick in the toilet. I begged her not to tell anyone, but Bobby found her with coke in her bag and he was about to slap her around so she said she had something important to tell him. Bobby went mental. The camera was due to be installed the following weekend. He told me to get rid of it. He didn't want anything ruining his little earner.'

Mary shook her head.

'That's when I knew I had to get out of there. I had the money I'd saved, so I just grabbed everything and caught a train back to Dundee. I was paranoid that Bobby had Oliver watching me, but after I'd been home for a few weeks I thought that I'd got away with it. No one at the club knew my real name apart from Candy, and she'd disappeared.

'Mum and Dad were brilliant. I stayed with them till the baby was born, then Dad helped me find this place. I thought I'd put it all behind me, but then Bernard decided to try and find me.'

'He obviously didn't know your real name, but how did he know you were from Dundee?' I asked.

'I've been thinking about that, and I think I know. We were watching TV one evening and there was a news report about the new Victoria and Albert museum being built in Dundee. Bernard made some remark like, "Why on earth would they build it in a town like Dundee?" and I said, "Why not Dundee? It's not such a bad place." He asked why I was defending Dundee and I said I wasn't. We never mentioned it again, but he must've remembered it.'

'Kagan gave me this story about Tavernier being an old friend who was helping him out,' I said. 'He said that he was due to be married, but then his fiancée found out about his affair with you and called off the wedding.'

Mary laughed bitterly. 'All lies. He's never been engaged, and I never had any affair with him. I wouldn't let that slug near me.'

'Which leads me to my next question. Who's Colin's father?'

'Lap dancers have a lot of free time during the day. I found a bistro not far from the flat and I used to go there a couple of times a week for lunch. The assistant manager was a young guy from New Zealand. His name was Ranald and he was tall with dark curly hair and a big smile. It was obvious that most of the girls who worked there – and a lot of the female customers – fancied him. But he seemed to like me, and I was flattered. We used to talk a lot, and we went to the movies a couple of times in the afternoon.'

Mary shrugged and smiled.

'I suppose you could say it was the first time I had a proper boyfriend. I never took Ranald to Bernard's flat, but he had a bedsit not far from the bistro and I went there a couple of times . . . and the inevitable happened.

'When I told him I was pregnant he seemed delighted. We actually started to make plans. He talked about marrying me and taking me back with him to New Zealand. A day or two later, I went to the bistro, but the manager told me that Ranald had called in to say that he quit. I tried calling his phone but it'd been cut off. He may have gone back to New Zealand, but he wasn't taking me.'

So Mary had told me the truth about her child's father.

'It's obvious that Tavernier made up the story that he was acting for a client,' I said.

'I don't know why for sure. Maybe he didn't want anyone asking why a man his age was trying to find a young woman and why, in the only picture he had of her, she was wearing a schoolgirl's uniform.'

I nodded. 'But here's the bit that worries me: Kagan knew that Tavernier had hired me. Not only that, but he knew the fee I'd agreed with Tavernier and that the judge had connections in Dundee. The only way he could've known that would be if Tavernier had told him, and I don't think the judge would've done that willingly.'

'You think that Bobby had something to do with Bernard's death?'

'The cops say that Tavernier died of a heart attack, but he'd been badly beaten first. I think that Kagan heard that Tavernier was looking for you and decided to find out what he had learned. I reckon Tavernier told Kagan about hiring me, but that's all. I hadn't had the chance to tell Tavernier I'd tracked you down. Kagan just went too far and the judge's heart couldn't take it.'

Mary's eyes grew moist. 'Poor old Bernard. He didn't deserve that. So, what do we do, Mr Linton?'

'Well, we could go to the police. But it's all a theory; there's no actual proof, and I'll bet that Kagan has a bomb-proof alibi for the time of Tavernier's death.'

'But Bobby came to see you. How does he explain that?'

'He could make up any story he wanted about coming to see me. He could say he was looking for a long-lost relative. It would be my word against his and he has Oliver to back him up. Plus, if we went to the cops, I'd have to tell them the whole story, which would mean telling them about you. Kagan could find out who you really are and where to find you.'

Mary slumped down in her seat. She looked beaten.

'That wouldn't be a problem for Bobby,' she said. 'Some of the girls at the club told me he had something on a couple of cops in London. They helped him out from time to time.'

'I told Kagan that I hadn't found Tina Lamont which, strictly speaking, is true. But I think he knows I'm not telling him everything. When I left the office to come here, he tried to follow me.' I saw the look of panic reappear and quickly went on, 'Don't worry, like I told you, I made sure that he couldn't follow me – or at least my colleague did. But Kagan won't give up. You ruined his plan to get a judge under his thumb. He wants you to pay for that.'

Mary was quiet for a moment before she said, 'You said it was time for me to start telling the truth, Mr Linton. Well, there's one more thing I have to tell you. When I left the club for the last time I took a bag of money with me. It was Bobby's money.'

Fuck, I thought. How much worse could this get?

'How much?'

'Just over £40,000.'

I closed my eyes and massaged my forehead. 'I think you'd better explain.'

'I'd gone to the club to make sure I hadn't left anything in my locker that might help them trace me. It was during the day and there was no one around. On the way out, I passed Bobby's office. The door was open and I peeked in, just to make sure he wasn't there. He wasn't, but there was a canvas bag on his desk. It was full of cash.'

'Did Kagan make a habit of leaving money around?' I asked.

'No, I don't know why it was there. Maybe someone had left it there for him. The club isn't Bobby's only source of income. He has money coming in from other businesses, always in cash. I'm fairly sure they aren't all legit. Anyway, I grabbed the bag and got the hell out of there.'

'What were you thinking of?'

Mary looked at me defiantly. 'I wasn't thinking. Bobby had been ripping me off, taking a cut of my tips. Okay, not forty grand, but I wasn't stopping to count out my share.' Her eyes narrowed in anger. She was breathing heavily. 'That evil bastard hit me and threatened me. And he told me to get rid of my baby.'

'I have to think about this,' I told her. 'In the meantime, I think you should call your folks and ask them if you and the wee lad can stay with them. I think it'd be best if you weren't alone for a while. You have a phone?'

When she nodded I said, 'Don't use it. Phones can be traced. I'll be back in a sec.'

I went out to my car, took a mobile from the glove box and went back in.

'This is a pay-as-you-go. It's loaded with plenty of call time. Use it to call your folks. It has my mobile number already on it. You can call me if you have to. Don't worry, it's just a precaution, but better to be safe than sorry. And

Mary, don't run away again. You might think that's the answer, but it won't help in the long run. We have to sort this once and for all. I'll try my best to help you.'

A small cry came from the bedroom.

'Your son needs you,' I said. 'And I need to speak to Niddrie. I'll contact you tomorrow.'

As Mary left to go to her child, she turned back to me. 'I'm trusting you, Mr Linton.'

I remembered Bruce McAllister saying pretty much the same thing. Trouble was, Bobby Kagan was a bigger problem than Nikki McKay. She just thumped people with a frying pan. People died when they crossed Bobby Kagan.

24

When I got back on the dual carriageway heading towards Dundee, I called Niddrie.

'How'd it go?'

'The bin men kept the Range Rover blocked in for another five minutes after you left. The English guys didn't make any attempt to follow you. They sat speaking, and then went off in the other direction. Did you speak to Mary?'

'I did. She called herself Tina Lamont when she lived in London. She also lied to us about not knowing Tavernier. But I think she's telling the truth now. The guy who argued with the bin men is called Bobby Kagan. He was Mary's employer in London. He's not a nice guy. I'm not going back to the office, but I'll meet you tonight and tell you the whole story. There's a pub in the Ferry called the Ferryman. I'll be there at seven. This is turning into a real mess, Niddrie.'

There was silence for a moment before Niddrie came back on.

'Right, but it's not all bad news,' he said.

'What do you mean?'

'I got some comfortable Y-fronts today, sixty per cent off. See you at seven.'

When I got back to the Ferry I drove around for a bit but

there was no sign of the Range Rover, so at least Kagan hadn't found my address ... yet. I parked the Hyundai and went up to my flat.

I didn't feel like cooking, so I made a sandwich. Nothing too complicated, just some cold chicken, ham and coleslaw. As an afterthought, I added a pickled egg I found in the fridge and a packet of salt and black pepper crisps to the plate. All washed down with the drink made from discarded parts of the Tay Rail Bridge. Dealing with bad boys from down south, you have to keep your strength up.

At 6.55 p.m., I left the flat. I looked both ways when I reached the street, but there was still no sign of Kagan and his chum. If they had confronted me, I'd have just breathed on them. That would have given me enough time make my getaway before they recovered.

The Ferryman wasn't one of my usual haunts, but I dropped in for a pint now and again and I knew it wouldn't be busy on a Monday evening. Niddrie and I arrived at the door at exactly the same time, bang on 7 p.m. We went in and I ordered a couple of pints of Ossian's, which is brewed just twenty miles away in Perth, and took our drinks to a booth at the back. We were the only two customers in the bar.

Over the next half hour I told Niddrie about the visit from Kagan and Oliver. Then I went over every detail of my meeting with Mary Pigott. He didn't say a word, just sipped his beer. When I had finished talking, I asked, 'Well, what d'you think?'

Niddrie pursed his lips and nodded a couple of times. Then he spoke. 'Well, now we know how the judge knew for a fact that Mary's really a brunette. I think we can assume that Kagan didn't believe you when you told him that you

187

hadn't found Tina. Wait, this is getting bloody confusing. Let's just call her Mary from now on. That's why he dangled that five grand in front of you. My guess is that he was pretty sure you'd try to earn that money. For a start, you'd go to Mary to tell her that someone from London had turned up and was looking for her. That's why he was waiting to follow you. Once he knew where Mary lived ... Well, I don't think he intends to kiss and make up. Kagan isn't an idiot. He'll have worked out that you deliberately stopped him from following you. Ironically, that kind of confirms you know where Mary is.'

'I think you're right. But, on the subject of names, why did Kagan tell me his name was Nash?'

'Kagan isn't a common name. Maybe he thought there was a chance you'd recognise it. Actually, I looked online before I came. There are hints that he has his fingers in some dodgy but profitable pies. Nothing that connects him directly with any criminal activities, but it's pretty clear he isn't in the running for Philanthropist of the Year. You told Mary that you thought there was no point in going to the police, and I agree. So, we come down to the options. The first is: you tell him where to find Mary and pick up five grand.'

Before I could say anything, he held up a hand.

'Okay, I know you; that's not going to happen. The second option is that we persuade him to go home and forget about Mary. But Kagan's seriously pissed off. He thought he was going to have a judge in his back pocket before Mary ran out on him. He could've raked in some serious money from that. And that's before you take into account the £40,000 she took.

'So, he's going to take a lot of persuading. I could show

him my adjustable spanner, but he isn't some schoolboy rugby player. I think it's going to take more than that to convince him that the best thing he can do is to get in his Range Rover and head back south. Do you want another pint?'

'No, thanks. I think I'll go back to the flat and see if I can come up with some sort of compromise – one that'll be acceptable to someone whose main negotiating tool is a psycho with a bottle of acid.'

'Could be a tricky one,' admitted Niddrie. 'As Sundance said to Butch, "You just keep thinking. That's what you're good at." And if I think of anything, I'll let you know.'

I looked at Niddrie. I never knew he was a fan of old movies.

I said, 'Thing is, I don't think we have a lot of time. I have a feeling we'll be hearing from Mr Kagan sooner rather than later.'

We didn't have long to wait.

25

I spent the next few hours trying to think of a way to get Kagan to leave Mary Pigott and her child alone. The obvious thing was to get the £40,000 from Mary and give it back to Kagan. But I didn't know if she still had the money. She could have spent the lot. And even if she hadn't spent a penny, I was sure that wouldn't satisfy Kagan. To his twisted way of thinking, he had been robbed of a lot more than that. Mary had shown him a lack of respect, and for that she would have to pay.

Mary had been stupid and got in way over her head, but she didn't deserve to be hounded by a vindictive piece of shit like Kagan. Niddrie had been right; there was no way I would give her up. Trouble was, if Kagan couldn't get his hands on Mary, he would take it out on the person who was protecting her. My dad had always told me to do what's right. Sometimes I wish he had kept his advice to himself. No, sorry, Dad, on second thoughts, you were right.

Niddrie and I had arranged to meet in my office at 10 a.m. and I got there a few minutes early. I was sure I had locked the door when I left yesterday, but now it was ajar an inch. I entered and found a smiling Bobby Kagan in my chair. Oliver was looking out of the window. He didn't turn round.

'Ah, here you are, Mr Linton. Hope you don't mind, but

we got a bit tired of waiting for you and let ourselves in.'
Kagan gestured over his shoulder at Oliver. 'My colleague
is a man of many talents. It's amazing what he can do with
just a little flick of a knife.'

'What do you want?'

'You know what I want. I think you haven't been entirely
truthful with me, Mr Linton. After that little stunt with the
bin lorries – that was nicely done, by the way – you went to
speak to Tina. I want you to tell me where she is.' He swept
an arm round the room. 'We've had a good look round,
but we didn't find any paperwork referring to your search
for Tina.'

It's just below you, I thought, behind three inches of steel,
but I don't think Oliver would get through that with a flick
of his knife.

'We could go through your computer, but that'd be time-
consuming and, frankly, I've had just about enough of this
place. So, let's get on with it. Where is she?'

'And if I don't tell you?'

Kagan picked up the photo of Ailsa from my desk. He
smiled. 'Your daughter? I recognise the uniform. She's at
that school just along the road, isn't she? I think I saw her
going in earlier this morning. Oh, she's lovely ... Beautiful
skin.' He turned and showed the photo to Oliver. 'Doesn't
she have lovely skin, Oliver?'

Oliver looked at the photo. Behind me, the door opened
and Niddrie walked in.

'Sorry I'm late,' he said cheerfully. 'Traffic was murder.
Bloody cyclists slowing everything down. Not interrupting
anything, am I?'

Kagan replaced the photo and rose out of my chair. 'No,
we were just about to go. Think about what we discussed,

Mr Linton. You have my number. Call me when you've reached a decision. I'll give you till tomorrow at noon.'

Niddrie stood aside to let them pass through the door. As they left, Oliver looked at him as if he wanted to get into a pissing contest. Niddrie looked like he couldn't give a fuck.

'He's started making threats,' I said to Niddrie after they had gone and I'd reclaimed my chair.

'Thought that would happen.'

'Not against me directly. Ailsa.'

'I can do this one of two ways,' said Niddrie. 'I could follow the psycho and stop him before he can do anything, but I think he's the kind who could spot a tail. Or I can follow Ailsa. She'd never realise I was there. I think that's the way to go. I won't let anything happen to her, Allan.'

'I know that.'

'Do you have any ideas?'

'One or two. First I have to speak to Mary.'

I called the phone I had given her. She answered on the third ring.

'Is everything all right?' I could hear the edge in her voice.

'I've spoken to Kagan. Don't worry, I haven't told him where you are. I'm trying to persuade him to end this. For a start, we have to give him back the money. Have you still got it?'

There was a pause before Mary answered. 'There's just over £35,000 left. I had to pay for rent, food and clothes. And remember, some of that was mine anyway.' She sounded defiant.

'That's okay. I can't come and collect the money myself in case Kagan tries to follow me. But I have an idea. I'll call you back in five minutes.'

I rang off and turned to Niddrie.

'Your friend in the library – think she'd help us out?'

I explained, and Niddrie said there was only one way to find out. He used the speed dial on his mobile. She answered right away.

'Hi, Claire,' Niddrie said. 'I've a favour to ask.'

A few minutes later, Niddrie came off the phone and said, 'No problem.'

I called Mary.

'Here's what I want you to do,' I told her. 'Ask your dad to drop off the bag with the money at the central library after 10 a.m. tomorrow morning. Tell him to ask for Claire. She'll be expecting it.'

Mary said she would do as I asked. I came off the phone and turned to Niddrie.

'I think that Ailsa will be safe while she's in school. I want you to collect the bag and put it in the boot of my car. I'll give you my spare key. I won't park in the usual place in case Kagan has someone watching my car. There's a car park in the West Port. I'll leave it there.'

I paused and looked at Niddrie.

'You don't think I'm being over cautious?'

Niddrie shook his head. 'In the Pay Corps we prepared for any and every eventuality. You can never be too careful. Kagan said you had till noon tomorrow, but I don't believe a word that comes out of that bastard's mouth. He may just decide to jump the gun. I think I'll wander along to Ailsa's school and check things out. She'll be coming out for lunch soon.'

Niddrie left the office. I had no doubt that he would stop Oliver from getting anywhere near Ailsa, but what if Kagan had sent for reinforcements? Did I risk Ailsa being scarred for life, or – even worse – did I do what Kagan wanted and tell him where to find Mary?

The door of my office opened and the best-dressed man I knew walked in.

'Hello, Michael,' I said.

26

Michael Grant sat in the chair opposite me and looked round the room. As ever, he was expensively and immaculately clothed. My mind flashed back to the day we first met and the little boy in a patched-up jersey and trousers that were two sizes too big.

'It's okay,' I said. 'The place isn't bugged.'

Michael smiled. 'I didn't think it would be, Allan. I was just thinking that I've been back in Dundee for a few years now, but this is the first time I've been to your office.'

'Well, if you need my services, Michael, I'd be happy to help you, but I'm a bit busy at the moment.'

Michael leaned forward and looked at me very seriously. 'That's what I feared. With a gentleman from London?'

I wasn't expecting that one. Michael saw the look on my face and nodded. 'So, I take it you've met this person?'

'Yes,' I replied. 'He's been to see me.'

'Okay. I have to tell you something, Allan. It's important. A few weeks ago you asked if I could help you track down a young woman called Tina Lamont.'

'You called me back later and said you couldn't help.'

'At the time, that was correct. I'd called some of my contacts both here and down south, but they'd never heard of her. However, I was in Manchester yesterday – a combination of business and pleasure. Last night I had dinner with a business acquaintance and, as it happens, one of the people I'd previously contacted to ask about this Tina Lamont.

'My acquaintance happened to mention that recently she'd been in London, where she'd heard a rumour that someone was looking for a girl who used to work for him but had run off back to Scotland.'

'Bobby Kagan.'

'That's right. My dinner companion didn't know all the details, but she wondered if this could be the young woman I'd been enquiring about a few weeks ago. Then, she advised me most strongly not to get involved with Bobby Kagan. I asked her why not and, after some persuasion, she told me.'

'I know that he runs a lap dance club in London and that not all his business interests are strictly legitimate.'

'Actually, Allan, he owns a string of clubs throughout the south-east of England. But they're just a front. Most of his money comes from people trafficking, in particular young women from Eastern Europe. They're brought into this country and put to work in brothels in which he retains a major stake. He also has a lucrative sideline in bringing in firearms from the same part of the world.'

'No drugs?'

Michael wasn't embarrassed by my question.

'My acquaintance wasn't sure,' he said. 'I've certainly never come across him before, but I tend to stay out of the south. Too many unstable characters down there. Anyway, despite all this, Kagan's never been charged with anything. The story is that he has a couple of officers fairly high up in the Met on his payroll. They've been helpful to him in that respect.'

'He was trying to use Tina to blackmail a judge,' I said. 'That's why she did a runner.'

'Hmm. Hard to blame her. Maybe it's time you told me how you got involved in this.'

So, I gave him the whole story, starting with the day a man calling himself Carter came into my office, and leaving out only Mary's real identity and where she was now.

When I was finished Michael said, 'This other guy, Oliver. My acquaintance mentioned him too. He's devoted to Kagan. It's some kind of psychosexual attraction. Kagan isn't gay – far from it apparently – and there hasn't actually been any kind of sexual relationship, but Kagan plays on it and Oliver will do anything for him, literally anything.'

'I think Oliver beat up the judge when they were trying to find out what he knew about Tina. They've also threatened to get to me through Ailsa. This Oliver seems to specialise in beating up old men and throwing acid at women. Niddrie's keeping an eye on Ailsa just now.'

'I think you can take it that Oliver does more than beat up old men and mutilate women, Allan. People who've fallen foul of Kagan have turned up dead with a bullet in the head.' He looked at me earnestly. 'You say that Kagan's given you until tomorrow at noon to get in touch. What are you going to do?'

I thought for a minute.

'I'm going to arrange a meeting with him. I'll give him back the money that Tina took, at least most of it.'

'That won't be enough for Kagan. You know that.'

Michael looked up at the ceiling, but I don't think he was admiring the cornice. Then he made a decision and looked back down at me.

'Oliver will be armed, and probably Kagan too,' he said.

'I don't encourage my people to get involved with guns, but I have a contact in the west of Scotland. He can provide armed protection. It'll take a couple of days to organise and I'll pay for it. Try and stall Kagan till then.'

'Kagan is running out of patience. I don't think I can risk that, Michael.'

'The last thing my acquaintance said to me was, "If Kagan doesn't get what he wants, someone always suffers." I know that things have changed between us, Allan, but I still think of you as my best friend. So, I'm begging you. Give him what he wants.'

'Thanks, Michael, I do appreciate you coming here, and I'll give some serious thought to what you've said.'

Michael got to his feet and I accompanied him to the door.

With his hand on the doorknob he stopped and turned to face me. 'I'll give you this promise, Allan. If anything happens to you, somehow I'll make Kagan pay.'

'You daft bugger. You sound like a character in one of those old black and white movies from the forties. Behave yourself.'

'Well, that's your fault. You used to make me watch them when we were kids.'

I put my hand on his shoulder and smiled. 'When this is all over, let's have dinner. My treat. I've found a great little Italian restaurant up the Perth Road. The owner's a real character.'

'I'd like that.'

Michael turned and walked down the stairs. I thought, I have two friends who would stand beside me no matter how much shit hit the fan. One is a major drugs dealer who had just offered to hire a gunman to protect me, and the other claims to have been in the Pay Corps and goes around with a monkey wrench in his pocket scaring teenagers. I'm a lucky guy.

I sat down at my desk and opened my computer. I thought for a few minutes, then started typing. When I had finished, I printed out the pages and sealed them in an envelope. Then I phoned George.

'Can you spare me a few minutes?'

'No problem. Come along to the office.'

'I'll be there in ten minutes.'

I called Niddrie.

'How's it going?' I said.

'Fine. Ailsa came out for lunch. Jeez, that girl can eat! Where does she put it?'

'Just be grateful you don't have to buy her breakfast.'

'Anyway, she's back in class. No sign of Kagan or that weirdo but I'll be here when school comes out.'

'Ailsa usually goes to her grandmother's after school,' I informed him, 'but sometimes she goes to Hannah's office and they go home together.'

'Whatever, I'll make sure she's safe.'

I ended the call, picked up the envelope and left the office. When I got down to the street I took my time having a good look around. There was no sign of anyone who looked like a people trafficker from London, so I started walking.

Reform Street was completed in 1832 and was named after the Great Reform Act, which gave Dundee an MP for the first time. It was specifically designed as a shopping district. My dad said it used to be one of the busiest streets in the city. But over the years the shops closed and the street became lined with banks and building societies. Now, even they've disappeared. There's a place where you can buy umpteen different kinds of expensive coffee and a fast food outlet with a good Scottish name that actually originated on the other side of the Atlantic. I shun them both.

But, hidden away in the two-centuries-old buildings, several law firms have their premises in the street. They are like rabbit warrens, with steep stairs and narrow corridors leading to offices large and small. I suppose the size of the room depends on your status in the firm. George's office was somewhere in the middle.

I knocked on his door and went in. He rose from behind his desk and beamed at me.

'Where the fuck have you been hiding? We haven't had a pint in bloody ages!'

That's the thing about lawyers: they have such a delicate grasp of the English language. Must be all that addressing the jury.

George indicated the visitor's chair and sat down.

'Sorry, mate, been a bit busy,' I said.

'No worries. What can I do for you?'

I placed the envelope on his desk.

'I want you to look after this for me for a few days. All being well, I'll get it back from you unopened.'

George picked up the envelope and studied it. I had handwritten his name on it.

'Sounds serious, Allan. Can I ask what it's about?'

The letter inside contained a brief account of my being hired by Bernard Tavernier and the subsequent meetings with Bobby Kagan. I had kept details to a minimum, not naming anyone else. It ended with a declaration that I was going to meet Bobby Kagan and an employee of his known as Oliver, specifying the time and place.

'I can't tell you at the moment, George. But if I don't

come back for it in the next few days, I want you to take it to the police.'

George dropped the envelope on his desk and sat back in his chair. Now he looked worried.

'Hang on a minute, Allan. What the hell's going on here?'

'It's just a precaution. Probably worrying about nothing. You will do it, won't you?'

'Of course. But . . .'

I stood up.

'Don't worry, mate. I'll see you in a couple of days and we'll go for that pint.'

I left the office and returned to my car. I had done all I could do for the moment, so I drove home.

That evening I called Ailsa on her mobile.

'What's up, Dad?' she said. 'Calling me for dating advice?'

'I take it your mother isn't within earshot?'

'No, I'm in my bedroom. So, ask away.'

'Can't a dad just phone his daughter for a chat?'

'Of course, but I still have to give you some advice. Call Miss Morrison. One of the maths teachers, Mr Galloway, has been trying to chat her up. He's a creep, but if you keep her hanging on, his horrible chat-up lines might just work. I thought I was going to throw up when I heard him today. Saying he was thinking of going to France on holiday and asking if she could give him French lessons. Yuck!'

'Okay, I promise to call her in the next couple of days and rescue her from the odious Mr Galloway.'

'Good thinking, Dad. Is there something else I can help you with? Anything except advice on what you should be wearing. You're a bit of a lost cause, fashion-wise.'

'No, I think I can manage to struggle on without the help of my personal life coach.'

I could hear Ailsa giggle.

'Cool. Oops, got to go, Dad. Got another call coming in. It's Kirstie. Love you.'

I hung up with a smile on my face. She had lifted my heart. There was no way I was going to let anyone harm a hair on my little girl's head. I made one more call, and then I went to bed.

27

The next morning, I drove into the city centre, parked in the West Port and walked to my office. At 10.30 a.m. I called Niddrie.

'How is everything?' I asked when he picked up.

'No problems. Hannah dropped Ailsa off at school. I collected the bag from Claire and put it in the boot of your car. I'll be here when Ailsa gets out at lunch.'

'When this is all over, you should take Claire out for dinner as a way of saying thanks.'

There was a pause before Niddrie said, 'Who says I haven't thought of that already?'

At 11 a.m. I called the number Kagan had given me. He answered on the second ring.

'Ah, Mr Linton. Good to hear from you. I take it you've reached a decision?'

'Yes, I have, Mr Kagan.'

Kagan chuckled at my use of his name.

'Ah, so now you know who I am. Then you'll also know of my reputation. I'm a man who likes to get his own way. Where's Tina Lamont?'

'I've spoken to Tina and she has something of yours she wants to give back. She wants to speak to you personally, try to explain things. She's living out in the countryside, not far from Dundee. You can meet her there. I can give you directions. It's pretty isolated and you won't be disturbed.'

'Excellent! I knew you'd see sense in the end. I'm afraid I can't pay you the £5000, though. I've had to go to an awful lot of extra expense.'

'Okay, I understand. I just want this thing to be over.'

'It will be. Now, these directions?'

I gave him what he wanted and said that Tina would be there some time after 7 p.m. I rang off and sat back in my chair, hoping I had done the right thing.

About 12:30 p.m., Niddrie called me.

'Did you call Kagan?' he asked.

'Yes, he says that something's come up that he has to deal with. I don't think it has anything to do with Mary. He says he'll call me back tonight.'

'Okay, then I'll stick with Ailsa. She's just come out of school. Let me know what happens when Kagan calls back.'

I said I would and we ended the call. I thought about what I had just done. I had never lied to Niddrie before and I hated doing it now, but on this one occasion , I thought it would be better if he wasn't involved.

I made another call, which lasted about twenty minutes. Then I sat back and went over everything I had said and to whom I had said it. I thought I'd got everything right. Mind you, I think Herr Hitler had thought pretty much the same thing when he'd gathered his generals round the map table and said, 'I've had this great idea, lads. Don't worry, I've thought it through and nothing can go wrong. Let's invade Russia.'

I decided I needed some fresh air, so I left the office and wandered about the city centre till I found myself at the entrance to the central library. Claire was at the desk.

She smiled at me and I went over.

'Hello,' she said. 'You're ... er ... Niddrie's friend.'

'That's right. My name's Allan.'

We shook hands.

'I just thought I'd come and thank you for helping us out,' I said.

'It was nothing.' She looked at me hesitantly then said, 'Actually, I'm glad you came in. There's something I'd like to ask you.'

'Fire away.'

'Well, it's kind of a silly question, but what's Niddrie's name? I mean, is Niddrie his first name or his second name?'

I had to smile.

'I don't know. I've only ever called him Niddrie. To be honest, it's never seemed to matter. Why don't you just ask him?'

'No, it's all right. If that's what you call him then I'll do the same.' She paused then went on, 'Niddrie's nice, isn't he?'

'Nice' wasn't an adjective I ever thought I would hear applied to Niddrie.

'My daughter really likes him,' I said. Claire's face clouded over, so I quickly added, 'She's only fifteen and she calls him Uncle Niddrie.' Claire relaxed and I smiled. 'You like him too, don't you?' She nodded her head shyly and I said, 'I think it'd be a good idea if he asked you out.'

As I turned to leave I added, 'I'm working on it.'

She beamed at me.

I drove home. I parked and took the bag from the boot and carried it up to my flat. I tipped the money on to my table and counted the notes. Mary was right. There was £35,780, mainly in fifty and twenty-pound notes. I stuffed them back in the bag and settled down to wait.

At 6.30 p.m. I returned the bag to my car boot. I drove out of the Ferry and on to the Kingsway. What passes for rush hour in Dundee was over and I was soon at the big junction, waiting for the lights to change so that I could turn right onto the dual carriageway which led to Forfar.

Fifteen minutes later, I turned off the Forfar Road on to a B-road. It twisted and turned for several more miles till I saw a track leading down to a cottage. I drove past the track till I reached a gravelled layby. I pulled in and parked the Hyundai. I got out and looked back down the track. It was early autumn, so there was still plenty of daylight, and I could clearly see a Range Rover with darkened windows parked in front of the cottage.

I took the bag from the boot and started down the track. As I neared the cottage, I could see that the door had been kicked in. I stopped a few yards from the door, just as Kagan emerged from it. Oliver was right behind him. He was wearing his long black coat. I put the bag down at my feet.

Kagan's face twisted in a snarl.

'What the fuck do you think you're playing at, Linton?' He jerked a thumb back at the door. 'This place is a dump. No one's lived here for ages. Where's that bitch?'

'I'm not telling you that.' I pointed to the bag at my feet. 'Here's the money she took from you. It's about five grand short. But, as you owe me that, we can call it even.' I shook my head. 'What's the point of going on with this? The judge is dead. You can't blackmail him now, so why don't you just take your money and go home?'

Kagan smiled at me, but I'm a detective and I could tell it wasn't a happy smile.

'Let me explain something to you, arsehole,' he said. 'Nobody fucks with me and gets away with it. Otherwise,

206

people will start to think I'm going soft. I can't have that.'

I nodded. Good to know Kagan was doing this on a point of principle and not just because he was a fucking psycho.

'The last person to try and stop me finding Tina was that old fool of a judge,' Kagan continued. 'Oliver spotted him trying to speak to some of the girls. They told Oliver that he was trying to locate Tina. He wanted to know if they knew where she'd gone. Of course they didn't. But I thought it still might be a good idea to have a quiet word with the judge – see if he'd been able to find out anything.

'Oliver knew where his flat was, so we went round to see him. He told us to clear off so, naturally, Oliver had to show him that it was in his best interests to cooperate.'

Kagan looked down at the ground, as though remembering.

'That took a bit longer than we expected,' he said. 'Got to hand it to the judge. He was a stubborn old bugger. But Oliver tends to get people to tell him what he wants to know and, in the end, the judge told us about you. We were just leaving when the old boy collapsed. We couldn't do anything, of course. We just had to leave him. Took his wallet and some other stuff to make it look like a robbery gone wrong.'

Kagan made it sound like just another day at the office. I glanced at Oliver. His expression was as dead-eyed as usual, but I noticed he'd unbuttoned his coat.

'If only he'd done what we asked from the start, none of that would've happened,' Kagan said. 'So, Linton, are you going to be sensible and tell me, or do I have to ask Oliver to show you how persuasive he can be? Your choice.'

I made one last attempt. 'Please, walk away now or this will not end well.'

Kagan sighed – a touch theatrically, I thought – and said,

'Another fucking hero. Okay, you asked for it. Oliver, his kneecap.'

Oliver reached into his coat and pulled out a pistol. I don't know very much about guns, but it was black, not too big and looked like an automatic. He stepped forward and took aim at my right leg.

There was a flat crack, which died almost as soon as I heard it. Oliver stopped suddenly, as if he had walked into a brick wall. He dropped the gun and staggered back a few feet before collapsing.

Kagan looked down at Oliver, then turned back to me, his eyes full of rage and confusion. He reached behind him and pulled out a gun that looked identical to Oliver's.

'The fuck! What the fuck!' he shouted.

He brought the gun up to bear on me, but he wasn't aiming for my legs. But then there was another crack and he was lifted off his feet. He managed to pull the trigger as he fell back, but the bullet flew up in the air.

Then there was silence.

I took a few steps forward and leaned over Kagan and Oliver. They were lying just a couple of feet apart. Oliver's coat had fallen open and a deep red stain was spreading over the front of his expensive suit. Kagan was wearing a pale-blue shirt under his jacket and there was a similar bloody stain soaking through it. I remembered what he had said a few moments ago. I couldn't do anything, so I just had to leave them.

I turned, picked up the bag and walked back to my car. I didn't hurry. When I reached the Hyundai, I locked the bag in the boot. I got in, did a three-point turn and headed back to Dundee. I didn't turn on the CD player. I didn't feel like listening to anything.

AFTERMATH

28

It was early spring when I got in the car and headed west along the Kingsway. As ever at this time of year, the central reservation was a blaze of yellow as the daffodils came into full bloom.

At the junction with Forfar Road I caught a green light and drove on through. I didn't bother to glance to my right.

I had the CD player on and the first chords of 'Start Me Up' came crashing through the speakers. I had read an interview with Keith recently and he was talking about the oldest rock and roll band in the world going on tour again. By the look of him, Keith would need jump leads to start him up. On the other hand, if Mick kept fathering kids he probably would need the money.

When I'd got back to my flat after what happened, I'd checked my phone, which had been switched off. There were two voicemails from Niddrie. That could wait till tomorrow.

I took the bag out of the boot and put it in the bottom of my wardrobe, then I went and soaked in the bath for half an hour. To be honest, I didn't feel anything. No remorse, no guilt. Maybe, I thought, that would kick in later. As it happened, it never did. Those bastards had threatened to hurt my little girl. They had also made two attempts to put a bullet in me.

When I came out of the bath, I dried off and put on an old sweater and jogging bottoms. Ailsa would have had a fit if she had seen me. Then I realised I'd had practically nothing to eat all day, so I found half a crusty loaf and scooped out the inside. I rubbed olive oil into the hollowed-out loaf then sliced open a big tomato and rubbed that in too. Then I added some salami, pastrami and turkey slices, along with half a tub of mixed olives.

There was no beer in the fridge, but I did locate a can of Scotland's other national drink. I took the lot to my armchair and started in. When I had finished, I thought it might be a good idea to see if I had any indigestion tablets in the bathroom, but I started to nod and fell asleep.

It was after 10 a.m. the next morning when I woke up, still in the chair. I had a quick shower, shaved and switched on my phone. There were two more voicemails from Niddrie, so I texted him to say I would see him in the office in an hour.

I checked out the radio and TV news, but there were no reports of dead bodies found between here and Forfar.

I called George to tell him to hold on to the envelope and that I would be in later that day to pick it up. He said to come in any time. He sounded relieved.

Then I called Michael.

'Everything worked out,' I said.

'What do you mean, "worked out"?'

'Kagan won't be bothering me or the girl again.'

'You're not telling me everything, Allan.'

'I'm telling you everything you need to know, Michael.

I'll be in touch again soon about the dinner I promised you.'

I made one last call to the phone I'd given Mary. I told her that it was over and I would be in touch again soon. I rang off before she could ask me anything.

When I walked into the office, Niddrie was sitting in the visitor's chair. He didn't have to break in; he had his own key. He didn't say anything, just waited for me to start talking.

'The problem with Kagan has been resolved,' I started. 'You don't have to look after Ailsa any more.'

'You're absolutely sure about that?'

'I am. We won't be hearing from Kagan or his well-dressed friend again.'

Niddrie looked thoughtful then said, 'Good.' He rose and walked to the door. ' I might just nip into the library. Doing some research.'

I was glad he had changed the subject.

'I spoke to Claire yesterday,' I said. 'Thanked her for helping out.'

'I hope you said nice things about me.'

'What makes you think we talked about you?'

Niddrie's cheeks twitched and he left.

I turned on the television just in time to catch the lunch-time local news. There was still nothing about unsavoury characters from London being found dead locally.

I went round to George's office, knocked on the door and went in. He was just finishing off a burger that looked about a foot deep, plus a pile of chips. All that witness questioning; these lawyer guys have to keep their strength up. I managed to grab a couple of chips before he demolished them.

He wiped his hands with a paper napkin before handing my envelope to me.

'You're not going to tell me what this is all about, are you, mate?' he said as I tucked the envelope into the inside pocket of my jacket.

I shook my head. 'No, it's better for everyone that I don't.'

'But you're okay? No problems?'

'Yeah, thanks, George. It was just a precaution. In the end it turned out there was nothing to worry about.'

George sat back in his chair and smiled.

'Great. Now, what about this pint? I was thinking we could meet in the WAG after work tomorrow.'

'Perfect. I'll see you there.'

As I left the office he called after me, 'Leave the car at home!'

I drove home and found a box of matches in a kitchen drawer. I stood over the sink, took the envelope from my jacket pocket and set fire to it. I washed the ashes down the sink.

I spent the rest of the afternoon switching between news channels, but either Kagan and his pal had managed to pull off the feat that only one other character in history has managed, or they were still lying undiscovered.

Early in the evening I thought I had better follow my daughter's advice before Dani succumbed to the silver-tongued Mr Galloway, so I called her number.

'Hi,' I said. 'Sorry I haven't called before now. It's been a bit hectic this week.'

I didn't expand on that statement. I wasn't sure how she would react if I told her I'd had a confrontation with some bad guys, which ended in bullets flying around. She probably thought tracing lost cats was the highlight of my working day.

'That's all right,' she said. 'I've been busy too. Exams coming up.'

'I was wondering if you'd like to meet up again this weekend. I can't manage tomorrow – meeting an old pal for a few pints – but how about Saturday?'

'Sorry, I'm going out with friends on Saturday night.' There was a pause, then she went on, 'You could join us if you like. We're going to the cinema at Dundee Contemporary Arts. It's a live showing of *Aida*, broadcast from the Royal Opera House.'

'To be honest, Dani, I'm not all that keen on opera.'

Actually, if it came down to a choice between having several teeth pulled and going to the opera, the latter might edge ahead, but not by much.

Dani laughed. 'I understand perfectly. And, if we are being honest, I am not a great fan either, but I promised a friend I'd go with her.'

'How about Sunday then? I could pick the restaurant this time.'

'I have a better idea. Why don't you come here and I'll cook dinner?'

That wasn't a better idea. That was a terrific idea. I stopped punching the air long enough to put on my most casual voice.

'That could work. Say around seven thirty?'

Dani laughed again. I liked to hear her laugh.

'Excellent. See you then.'

On Friday I left the car at home and travelled into the city centre by bus. I took a good look around when I boarded, but obviously word had got around the hoodie community that travelling by bus wasn't safe.

I got into the office and spent the next three hours doing routine stuff. There was still no news. Surely someone must have noticed a couple of bodies by now? Then Ailsa walked in carrying a pie and one of those long sandwiches stuffed with about twenty different types of meat. I pride myself on my observational skills, but I could detect no sign of any green stuff.

'I brought your favourite lunch, Dad,' she said, cheerfully. 'And a little something for myself.'

As I was performing my granddad's grease-draining ritual into a paper towel, I asked my daughter, 'Ever been tempted by your home town's signature dish?'

She had already demolished half her sandwich, but she paused long enough to pull a face.

'Are you serious? My body's a temple.'

When she had finished, she licked her lips and grinned at me.

'You're seeing Miss Morrison again, aren't you?'

'I may be.'

'You are! She's been grinning all morning, and I saw her give Mr Galloway the brush-off.'

'I think it's time you got back to school, young lady. You don't want to be late for class.'

She wolfed down the last morsel then skipped out of the door.

'I told you to ask her out, Dad. Any more advice, just ask. I'll keep you right. Love you!'

I watched Ailsa leave, full of life and so precious to me, and for the first time, I stopped and thought about what I had done.

216

I had spotted the derelict cottage the second time I had gone to see Mary. In fact, I had driven part of the way down the track before I realised it wasn't hers. It was remote, with hardly any passing traffic, so when it came to deciding on a place to meet Kagan, it seemed ideal.

But it was never my plan to lure Kagan into a trap. I had given Kagan a choice. He could have walked away, but he wanted to make someone suffer because, in his twisted mind, he had been cheated and shown a lack of respect. So, he had as good as killed Bernard Tavernier, and I had no doubt he would have killed Mary Pigott if he had found her. And if it meant hurting Ailsa to force me to give up Mary, he wouldn't have given it a second thought. I had come across some very nasty people over the years, but none of them were as evil as Bobby Kagan.

I didn't have to justify what I had done to myself or anyone else.

To my knowledge, only two people knew I had arranged to meet Kagan ... Niddrie and Michael Grant. I was sure that they wouldn't be making any calls, anonymous or otherwise, to the cops. Mary knew that Kagan had been in contact with me, but there was absolutely no chance she would go to the police.

There could be something else linking me to Kagan. Maybe he had told someone in London he was coming to meet me. I would just have to wait until he and Oliver were found.

I looked at my watch. It was 4.45 p.m., so I locked up the office and headed to the WAG.

Sandy Brackenridge greeted me, 'I've just put on a new barrel of Courage Directors Bitter. You'll have a pint.'

Hard to argue with that, and a few minutes later I was

enjoying the first mouthful. Another English ale. Did that make me some kind of traitor?

The door opened and I turned round, but it wasn't George. My ex-father-in-law entered, followed by his usual entourage. We ignored each other.

Seconds later, George arrived. I glanced down the bar. Sandy was standing patiently as one of Fergus's minions attempted to put together an order that seemed to consist mainly of mineral water and other unmanly drinks. I raised my chin and Sandy strode back to me. He didn't have to ask; he just started pouring another pint of Directors. I looked down the bar to where the minion was standing, looking askance. A small victory, but enjoyable nevertheless.

We took our drinks to a small corner table and sat down. George took a long pull at his pint, closing his eyes.

'Aah! I needed that.'

'Tough day at the coalface?' I asked.

George took another sip, then grinned at me. 'I was defending a lad accused of assault today. No angel, but I was sure he hadn't done it. The guy who claimed he'd been assaulted was in the witness box and the prosecutor asked him if the person who'd assaulted him was in the courtroom. It shouldn't have been too hard a question. My man was sitting where the accused always is.

'Anyway, this idiot takes a good look round and finally points to this bloke sitting in the public gallery. "That's him," he says. The prosecutor says, "Are you sure?" but before I could object, the sheriff said that was enough. The accused was free to go.'

George laughed, and I joined in. For the next hour, we reminisced about similar scenes we had witnessed in the courts. We were almost finished with our second pint when Sandy came over and plonked two plates laden with shepherd's pie in front of us.

'Looks like you two are intending to make a session of this,' he said. 'In that case, you'd better get something in your stomachs. This is on the house.'

The WAG served food till 7 p.m. It was basic pub grub, with pies of all kinds dominating the menu. But the portions were intimidating, and although the guys in the kitchen were never going to win some television cookery show, they knew exactly what their customers liked.

There was a story that a young lawyer from Edinburgh had come in once and asked which salads Sandy had. Sandy had pointed to the blackboard behind the bar, which listed all the food on offer, and asked the young man if he saw a salad. The lad from Edinburgh had peered at the menu and finally admitted he didn't.

'That's because there isn't one,' Sandy had growled.

As so often happens when old friends meet, George and I talked about the old days. George mentioned a name – Peter Hildrey.

'I don't recognise the name, George.'

George smiled and said, 'Remember that time you did your knight in shining armour act when Michael Grant was being picked on after school?'

'Yeah, and got a right doing for my trouble.'

George had been a year ahead of me at school. The following day in the playground, he had heard all about that wee idiot Linton diving in to help the weirdo Grant.

George grinned, 'From what I recall, one of the older boys was about to put the boot into Michael when you sent him flying. That was Peter Hildrey.'

I remembered it now, even after thirty years. The punches, the kicks, walking home with a bloody nose. My mother not being best pleased and telling me to stay away from Michael. My dad slipping me a few coins to get chips. You can't buy memories like those.

George roused me from my reminiscing. 'Well, I came across him in court a few weeks back.'

'Still beating up wee kids?'

George smiled happily. 'Actually, he was giving evidence against two lads who were accused of assaulting him. He'd pushed in front of some old guy in a pub. When the old lad complained, Hildrey shoved him. What he didn't know was that the old boy's two sons were behind him. They took Hildrey out the back door of the pub. Last I heard, Hildrey is still attending the dental hospital, and he's still walking with crutches.'

'What happened to the two sons?'

'They said that they'd followed Hildrey out of the pub to remonstrate with him.' George chuckled. 'That's the word they used – "remonstrate" – and he'd slipped and fallen. There were no witnesses; it was pretty much his word against theirs. Witnesses did say that Hildrey had been drinking and he'd pushed the old boy. The case was dismissed. I don't think even the prosecutor was all that bothered.'

'Good to hear that justice has been done ... even if it's about thirty years too late.'

When we were done with the reminiscing, we went on to setting the world to rights. It never fails to amaze me how several pints can endow one with wisdom, erudition and insight. Maybe if Granddad and Adolf had got together over a few beers, a lot of unpleasantness could have been avoided. But I believe the wee bastard was a teetotaller, which explains a lot.

We were just finishing our sixth pints, on the verge of total lunacy and ordering another round, when I sensed a large presence behind me. A hand clapped on my shoulder and a voice said, 'Mr Linton. You'd better come with me.'

I turned and looked up into the smiling face of Fiona, George's better half. Fiona is a specialist in the eye department at Ninewells Hospital. I used to joke that she needed her own eyes tested when she agreed to marry George.

George smiled blearily at his wife. 'Hello, darling. Is it that time already?' He turned to me and explained, 'My dearest kindly volunteered to come and pick me up at ten thirty.'

'I thought that was about as long as he could last without losing consciousness,' Fiona told me. 'And I think I'd better take you home as well, Allan.'

As we staggered out of the pub, Sandy called after us, 'And don't come back until you're sober.'

Then he winked at Fiona. 'But you're welcome at any time, Fiona.'

She beamed at him.

As a rule, if I stick to beer and don't mix my drinks, I don't suffer from hangovers. However, I do tend to move very slowly the next day. On Sunday morning I was back to normal.

Ailsa called me.

'I heard you were blootered on Friday night, Dad.'

'Who told you that?'

'I heard Granddad telling Mum that he'd seen you in the Wig and Gown and you were sinking the pints.'

I didn't remember seeing Fergus leaving. However, I knew he rarely stayed longer than 7 p.m., but that wouldn't stop him from jumping to conclusions.

'I was having a social drink with an old friend.'

'So, what were you doing last night?'

'I was recovering from the social drink.'

'Dad! I thought you'd be seeing Miss Morrison this weekend?'

'As a matter of fact, she's invited me to dinner at her place this evening.'

'Dinner at her place, eh?' Ailsa sniggered. 'Well, you do have to get a move on, Dad. You're still not getting any younger.'

'I had intended to make you my sole heir, but I'll be consulting a lawyer tomorrow morning to alter my will in favour of a donkey sanctuary.'

'Have a great time, Dad – and remember, act responsibly.'

She hung up, leaving me, as ever, with a grin on my face.

At 7.29 p.m., I rang the bell at Dani's flat. The door opened and she stood there, looking stunning. She wore jeans and a blue and white striped top and she had pulled her hair back in a little bun.

I held up a bottle of red wine and she took it from me.

'A Malbec, from Argentina,' she said, inspecting the label. 'Good choice. It'll go perfectly with the food.'

'Actually, I drove here tonight, so I won't have a drink.'

Dani grinned at me. 'Then neither will I. Come in.'

She led me through to the kitchen, where there was an old oak table set for two. The aroma coming from a pot simmering on the stove was delightful.

'It's boeuf bourguignon,' Dani said. 'Actually, there's a lot of red wine in it, but I don't think it would be enough to make you fail the breathalyser. I hope you'll like it. Please, sit.'

Dani ladled generous portions into bowls then placed them on the table, along with a basket of bread roughly broken into chunks.

It was delicious. The meat was tender and the gravy was rich and packed with flavour. Dani didn't hesitate to dunk the bread into it. She paused with a chunk halfway to her mouth.

'You can serve this with dumplings or even potatoes, but I think it works as well with just the bread. What do you think, Allan?'

I soaked a hunk of bread and put in my mouth. When I stopped chewing, I said, 'It'd be a sin to waste this gravy.'

I used the last piece of bread to mop my plate, managing to avoid dripping gravy onto my chin. Dani picked up the plates and carried them to the sink.

'Where did you learn to cook like that?' I asked.

'I picked it up here and there, mostly from when I lived in France. You know, there's a lot of nonsense written and talked about French food. Actually, most of the French people I met just like good food, properly cooked.'

'What about "nouvelle cuisine"?'

Dani laughed. 'If you served that stuff in most of the places I stayed, they'd throw it back at you! But I hope you can manage a little dessert.'

She opened the oven and brought out two individual chocolate sponges. She added a massive dollop of whipped cream to each and brought them to the table.

She broke open hers with her spoon and a thick brown liquid oozed out.

'Normally, the filling would be melting chocolate, but I prefer caramel.'

I'm not a great lover of desserts, but it was amazing.

Dani cleared the plates.

'Coffee?' she suggested. 'Go through to the living room and I'll bring it.'

The living room had a high ceiling and a large bay window from which you could see Fife over the river. Its size meant it could easily accommodate the big old-fashioned furniture, which included a couch in front of the fireplace. For a moment I commiserated with the poor removal men who had had to carry this stuff up three flights of stairs. If it was any consolation, the room looked amazing.

Dozing on a large beanbag in the corner was a pure white cat. I assumed this was Sacha. I'm not much of a cat person, but I reckoned I owed him one. If he hadn't decided to go walkabout, I'd never have met Dani.

I sat down. A few minutes later, Dani brought through a tray bearing a carafe, cups and saucers, sugar and cream. She placed it on a low table in front of the couch and sat down.

Over coffee we talked. She asked about my night with George and laughed when I told her.

'You British with your pints of beer. How can you drink so much of it? I tasted it once.' She made a face. 'It was dreadful.'

I asked her how she managed to sit through hours of a production set in Egypt, but with the characters wailing away in Italian.

'I believe it has a happy ending, though,' I said. 'With the lovers dying in each other's arms after being walled up in a tomb.'

Dani held up her hands. 'Okay, it's not what you would

call ... What's the phrase? Ah, yes, a bundle of laughs. So, now we are even. Touché.'

Then she looked quizzically at me.

'Wait a minute,' she said. 'You said you didn't like opera, so how come you know so much about it?'

'Ah, busted. Actually, I googled it before I came tonight, just in case we ran out of things to talk about.'

She punched me lightly on the arm.

'You idiot, Allan. We never run out of things to talk about.'

She was right, and it was just before 11 p.m. when Dani asked if I would like more coffee.

'No, I think it's time for me to go,' I said.

At the front door I turned to face her.

'Thanks for a brilliant evening.'

Dani looked up into my face, her expression serious.

'Allan, I've been in relationships before, but they've not ended well. Much of the problem has been that I've rushed into things. I think that you could become important to me, but I want to take it gradually. I hope you feel the same way.'

She stood up on her tip toes, took my face in her hands and kissed me. Wow!

'I think I can manage that,' I said.

As I started down the stairs, she called from the doorway, 'I won't open the wine till you come back. We can drink it then. And even if you bring your car, maybe next time you won't have to worry about being over the limit when you leave.'

She closed the door, leaving me thinking, did she just mean what I think she meant?

Forty minutes later, I was getting ready for bed. Out of

habit I had the TV news on. Once a newspaperman, always a newspaperman. I was just about to switch it off when the newscaster said breaking news was just coming in. The bodies of two men had been discovered just a few miles outside Dundee.

29

Mick had just finished telling me that it was only rock and roll but he liked it, when I joined the A9 at Perth and headed north. The CD player clicked over and Ry Cooder launched into 'Little Sister'. My mind went back almost seven months, to the morning after I heard that Kagan and Oliver had finally been found.

I had switched on the early morning news when I woke up, but there had been no further developments overnight. I knew from my time on the paper that it would be later in the day before the police started to release more information. So, I followed my usual routine and was sitting at my desk when Niddrie came in and sat opposite me. He didn't say anything.

'To quote you,' I said, 'I prepared for every and any eventuality. But I felt it best that these preparations didn't include you.'

Niddrie thought for a moment then nodded. 'Need to know. I can't think of any argument against that. Now, there's something you can help me with. You're a man about town, a bon viveur. Can you recommend a restaurant?'

'What kind of restaurant?'

Niddrie looked surprised.

'You mean there's more than one?'

I spent the next ten minutes describing the eating places that I liked in and around Dundee. When I began listing the curry houses, Niddrie held up a hand.

'Tried curry once, didn't care for it. Brings back unhappy memories. I was told at the time it was goat, but I noticed there was a distinct lack of small domestic animals in the vicinity.'

'What about Italian then? I went to a place up on the Perth Road recently. Vincenzo's. I can recommend it. Terrific food and not expensive.'

'Expense is no object. I have twenty quid burning a hole in my pocket.'

I looked at Niddrie. His cheeks twitched.

'I take it you're not intending to dine alone?' I asked.

'Need to know,' he said, straight-faced.

'Well, have a think about it, but if you're going at the weekend, I advise you to book. I think it may be quieter through the week.'

That evening, the deaths of Kagan and Oliver merited at least a full five minutes on all the main news channels. A farm worker had noticed the Range Rover when he was passing on his tractor on Friday morning, but he thought that someone might have been looking at the derelict cottage. It wasn't till Sunday evening, when he was driving past again and saw the Range Rover hadn't moved, that he thought to go and take a closer look.

The police confirmed that Robert Kagan and Oliver Philpott, both from London, had been shot. Philpott? No wonder he liked to be known only by his first name. Kagan was described as a businessman who was known to the Metropolitan Police. Oliver was described as his associate. Officers from the Met had been sent north to liaise with the local cops.

Over the next couple of days, the police established that the two men had registered at a hotel in Dundee, but under the name of Nash, using a cloned credit card. Following a television appeal by the police, some local cleansing operatives came forward to say that they had been in an altercation with Kagan. Some guy had told them that Kagan was a poll tax collector, but they were adamant that this wasn't a reason for them to kill him. The cleansing operatives gave descriptions of the mystery man with his height varying between five foot five and over six feet and his age between twenty and fifty. They all agreed he was wearing a parka with the hood up, so they couldn't see his face clearly.

The police were examining Kagan's phone, but I wasn't worried about that. I hadn't wanted Kagan to have my number, so I had bought a pay-as-you-go mobile to call him on when I set up the meeting. That phone was now in the River Tay.

But Kagan's phone, along with a tablet they found in the Range Rover, provided the cops with a whole lot more information that allowed the Met to apply for warrants. All of his clubs in the south-east of England were raided. This, in turn, provided evidence of people trafficking and the discovery of brothels as far apart as Bristol and Newcastle. The nightly news bulletins showed footage of the police breaking down doors and leading away terrified young women. The cops also found a cache of weapons, ranging from handguns to assault rifles.

Several arrests were made and two senior officers in the Met were suspended, pending further enquiries.

But no one was arrested for the killings. Several suspects were taken in for questioning, but all were released without charge. Kagan had a lot of enemies and the police were working on the theory that this was a gangland execution, but they were baffled by the fact that it had taken place in a remote corner in the north-east of Scotland.

On the following Monday, I was back in my office when the door opened and Michael Grant walked in and sat down in the visitor's chair.

'I had a visit from the police last week,' he said. 'They wanted to know if I'd ever had dealings with Bobby Kagan. I was able to tell them, truthfully, that I hadn't. Then they asked me where I was on the evening Kagan's murder.'

Michael smiled. 'I told them I was attending a charity event to raise money for the victims of domestic violence. When they asked if anyone could confirm that, I told them to ask the two most senior female police officers in Bell Street. They were sitting at the next table.'

Michael leaned forward, serious now. 'You said that you'd told me everything I needed to know. I appreciate that you were trying to keep me out of it, but I have to ask, will anything ever come back on you, Allan?'

'No, you don't have to worry about that, Michael.'

We talked for the next few minutes and I told him George's story about Peter Hildrey.

'You know,' he said, 'I remember Hildrey and the others. It'd be so easy to make them pay for what they did to you and me, Allan. But what would be the point? What's done is done. There's no point in dwelling on the past.'

As Michael got up to leave, I wondered if he was just referring to a schoolboy scrap thirty years ago.

'Michael,' I said, 'there is one thing you could do for me.'

That evening, I went to see Mary Pigott at her parents' house. I said I had to speak to her alone and she led me into a bedroom.

'As you'll have seen from the news,' I said, 'you'll never have to worry about Kagan again. But there's the question of the money you . . . let's face it . . . stole from him. I take it your parents don't know about it?'

Mary shook her head.

'You can't profit from this, Mary – it wouldn't be right – but I can hardly give it back. So, I've arranged for it to go to various charities which benefit women and children who've suffered domestic abuse.'

Mary smiled and said, 'Absolutely, Mr Linton. I don't want it.'

She showed me to the door and as I turned to say goodbye, she hugged me.

'Thank you, for everything. You've given my baby and me a second chance. I won't waste it.'

Not far from the Pigotts' house is Dundee's airport, and beyond that is a short stretch of road where you can park right next to the river. It was deserted when I arrived, except for a Jaguar. I parked behind it and opened the boot of the Hyundai. I took out Kagan's bag of money. As I approached the Jag, the driver got out.

'Mr Grant's expecting this,' I said.

The driver took the bag.

'I'll take it to him right away.'

I got into my car and drove home.

As the weeks went past, the story faded from the headlines and disappeared from the TV newscasts. It burst briefly into life again in the new year, when an array of Kagan's lieutenants and minions were convicted on various charges. It also emerged that ballistics had proved that bullets test-fired from one of the guns found at the scene of the killings matched those taken from corpses found at various locations in the south of England in recent years.

The team from the Met returned south, leaving the investigation in the hands of the local boys.

I kept my promise to Miss Laverty and called to tell her that I had solved the mystery of the missing girl. I said that I couldn't give her details, but that her help had been invaluable. She made me promise that if I ever had any other cases involving school uniforms, I would call her first. I gave her my word that I would.

Another promise I kept was to Michael. I took him to dinner at Vincenzo's. He loved the food, but passed on the wine. Michael's driver was taking me home, so I managed a half carafe. We talked about a lot of things, but never about Bobby Kagan or Michael's business.

As the weeks went past, I wondered if I would receive a request to help the police with their enquiries. What if Kagan had mentioned my name to one of those minions?

Then one night I was in the WAG with Niddrie. He was at the bar getting in a round when I heard two men talking at the next table. I glanced round and recognised them as two detectives based at Bell Street.

'Anything happening on the Kagan killing?' asked one.

'Nah,' said his companion. 'It's going nowhere. Between you and me, those bastards got what they deserved. No one's breaking their balls to find out what happened.'

One story did make the local papers in January. The son of a prominent local solicitor was hurt when his Mini Cooper skidded off the road and hit a wall. The road was icy, but the cause of the accident was the level of alcohol in Scott Clayton's blood.

I was reading the report out loud to Niddrie in my office.

'Says here that the Mini was a total write-off, but young Clayton suffered only a broken arm and concussion.'

'Lucky lad,' said Niddrie.

'Funny thing is that there's no mention of any drugs being found in the wreckage of the car.'

'That right?' replied Niddrie.

I turned off the A9 at Ballinluig and headed for Aberfeldy. Ry had given way to Buddy Holly and that amazing guitar intro to 'Listen to Me' came soaring out of the speakers.

A couple of weeks earlier, I had been in my office when I received a telephone call.

'This is Mr Fergus McKendrick's secretary, Mrs Mathers.

Mr McKendrick would like to have a word with you. He can spare you twenty minutes this afternoon after three o' clock.'

'You can tell McKendrick that if he wants to speak to me, he knows where to find me. I'll be here for the next hour. If he can't make it then he'll have to call to make an appointment.'

I hung up.

Ten minutes later, the door opened and my ex-father-in-law walked in and sat down.

'This is a personal matter and what we say to each other never leaves this room,' he said.

'Depends on what you have to say.'

Fergus heaved a sigh, paused, then started talking.

'Some months ago, an old friend came to see me looking for some advice.'

Then it dawned on me.

'Bernard Tavernier. You were his connection in Dundee.'

'Bernard and I were old friends from university.'

He paused. I could see this was difficult for him, but I had no intention of making it any easier.

'Bernard told me he was looking for this girl,' he continued. 'He was sure she came from Dundee and he wanted to know if I could recommend someone to ... to help him. He told me how he'd met this ... Tina ... and how he'd set her up in his flat. I told him he was being a fool – a stupid, infatuated old fool. I knew it couldn't end well, so I gave him your name.' Fergus looked pleadingly at me. 'There was so little to go on. I thought you'd fail and that he'd give up on this madness.'

Fergus lowered his gaze then looked up again.

'Then I heard that Bernard was dead. At first I believed

what it said on the news, that he'd died during a robbery. Then those two criminals from London were found murdered just a few miles from here. I read in the paper that the man, Kagan, owned' – Fergus's mouth twisted in distaste – 'some kind of club. Bernard had told me that he first met Tina in a club. It was the same club.

'I tend not to believe in coincidences, Linton. I suspected that there could be a link between Bernard's search for this girl and the murders, but I decided not to go to the police. What was the point? Bernard was dead and so were those scumbags, most probably killed by their own kind. Bernard's wife, Caroline, has been through enough. She knows nothing about Bernard's involvement with this girl. If it became public knowledge, it would destroy her.'

Fergus seemed to think for a few moments before going on. 'You're no fool, Linton. I think you've made the same connection. You could've made a lot of money going to the papers with this story, but you've kept quiet.'

I wondered just how much Fergus knew about his old friend's relationship with Mary. Not too much, I suspected. I wasn't going to enlighten him.

'When I agreed to look for the girl, I promised Tavernier absolute confidentiality,' I informed him. 'That still stands.'

Fergus looked at me and pursed his lips.

'I appreciate that,' he said. 'After you met Bernard he came to see me again. He told me that he'd paid you a retainer and that he'd pay you another sum when you found the girl.'

Fergus reached into the inside pocket of his jacket and pulled put a slim white envelope.

'This is a banker's draft for that sum.'

I held up a hand.

'I don't take bribes, Fergus. I told you, whatever I know about your friend will remain confidential.'

'This isn't a bribe. You were hired to do a job. I don't know if you found this Tina and, frankly, I don't care. But I believe you've fulfilled your obligations to my old friend. I contacted the executors of Bernard's estate and told them you'd carried out some work for him, but you were never fully compensated before he died. They know me well and were willing to take my word. This is from Bernard, not from me.'

He put the envelope on my desk. 'As far as I'm concerned, this is rightfully yours. You've earned it.'

Fergus got up and went to the door. He paused and, without looking back, said, 'Bernard was the cleverest man I ever met – a double first at Cambridge. But even the brightest can make such fools of themselves when they think with their cock instead of their brain.'

He went out and closed the door behind him.

Seconds later, Niddrie appeared in the doorway. He jerked his thumb over this shoulder.

'I passed Ailsa's granddad on the stairs. What did he want?'

I held up the envelope.

'He brought me this. Bernard Tavernier has settled his account.'

'It's amazing what you can do with online banking these days.'

I had passed through Aberfeldy and was crossing the old stone bridge built by General Wade in the 1730s. Wade had built roads throughout the Highlands after the first Jacobite rebellion in 1715 to bring peace and tranquility to the land. I'm not sure how well that worked out because it had all kicked off again in 1745. Been fairly quiet since, although I've heard it gets a bit lively in Aberfeldy at closing time on a Saturday night.

Ten minutes later, I was climbing into the Perthshire hills. I had passed the turn-off to the village of Dull – which, I believe, is twinned with Boring in Oregon. Honestly.

I came out of a series of Z-bends and saw, up ahead, a single cottage situated on the hillside. I left the road and gingerly navigated the Hyundai up a track dotted with potholes – one of which, I'm sure, would have swallowed my little Korean whole. I pulled up in the yard in front of the cottage beside a dark-green Land Rover Defender, the vehicle of choice amongst much of Scotland's gamekeeping fraternity. I had once asked a gamekeeper why this was and he had replied with a grin, 'Because they're good at pulling all those poncey so-called "four-wheel drives" out of ditches.'

A man came out of the cottage carrying two mugs of tea. He was medium height, in his thirties, and the only man I knew who looked fitter than he did was Niddrie. He wore boots laced up over camouflage trousers and a checked shirt with the sleeves rolled to his elbows. The sun was shining, but it wasn't all that warm and I had kept my jacket on. I'd called ahead to let him know I was coming.

'Perfect timing, Allan. I've just made a brew.'

We carried the mugs over to a seat carved out of a tree trunk and sat down. I sipped the tea carefully. The first time I'd had a mug of Alec McMurdo's tea, I had taken a huge swig. It had been strong enough to strip paint and scalding hot. It was a mistake I didn't make twice.

Alec was the head keeper on an estate covering over twenty thousand acres of Perthshire. I had met him while I was still working on the paper, writing a series of articles on rural crime. There were the usual problems of poaching and rustling of farm animals, but also the theft of expensive machinery.

Perhaps more seriously, city criminals saw gamekeepers as a source of firearms. One keeper had returned home to find that some lowlifes had almost demolished an entire wall of his cottage in an attempt to get at his gun cabinet. They hadn't succeeded.

Alec had been a big help to me, giving me background details and introducing me to other keepers and farmers. We'd kept in touch, but this was the first time I'd visited him in several months.

On the other side of the yard was a row of kennels. Dogs of various breeds were dozing in the sunshine. A boy in his late teens with blond hair cut very short was playing with some Jack Russell puppies while the bitch kept an eye on things. The young lad turned round, smiled and gave me a wave.

'How's Davie doing these days?' I asked.

'Great. He's attending college in Perth, doing well. He won't follow me into the keeping though. Wants to become an engineer. Make himself some real money.

'He's been getting help and he swears to me he hasn't touched anything since he came back, and I believe him. To be honest, we just take it one day at a time.'

Davie is Alec's younger brother. When their parents had been killed in a crash on the A9, Alec had brought the boy up on his own. It hadn't been easy.

People think that drugs are only a problem in cities.

They aren't. Kids in rural areas can get their hands on just about anything they want. Alec had done his best, but the demands of his job meant that he wasn't always there for his brother.

It was an old but familiar story. Davie had started on weed and moved on to the harder stuff. To pay for it, he had started stealing from their cottage. Alec had gone ballistic when he found out what was going on. The truth was, he just didn't know what to do in that situation.

One day, Alec had come home to find Davie gone. He had reported it to the police, but they'd treated it as missing person case. There was no evidence that a crime had been committed.

After a few weeks, Alec had called me. He'd heard that I was now working as a private investigator and had asked if I could help.

'I don't have much money,' he said. 'But I'll give you what I've got. Just find my wee brother.'

I refused to take a fee, just enough to cover my expenses.

I started by asking around Davie's friends. After managing to convince one of them that I meant no harm to Davie, she told me that she'd had a text from him. He was in London and doing great.

Not many seventeen-year-olds go to London and become an overnight success. I'd written about runaways before and I had a sinking feeling in my stomach that I knew what had happened to Davie.

I knew the places to look and it took me little over a week to find him, on his knees in front of some sleazebag of a politician. I had never told Alec the exact circumstances in which I had found Davie.

When I had brought Davie back to the cottage, Alec had

hugged him, then looked over his shoulder at me with tears in his eyes.

'If there is anything I can do for you, Allan – anything – don't hesitate.'

When I had set up the meeting with Kagan, I had also called Alec. I explained the situation and that I needed someone to cover my back, hopefully only as a precaution. It was a lot to ask, and I would understand if he couldn't do it.

Alec had answered right away, 'Tell me where and when.'

Now, leaning back against the bench, I sipped my tea again. 'And how are you, Alec?'

Alec turned to me, a grin on his face.

'I know why you're here, Allan, but you don't have to worry about me. All these months and I haven't given it a second thought.'

'I have to admit I've been worrying about it. For a start, could the gun be traced back to you?'

Alec chuckled and clapped me on the shoulder.

'You've been watching too many cop shows on the telly. I'm fairly sure there's no such thing as CSI Aberfeldy. Let me put your mind at rest. A few years back we were having a problem with poachers. Some of the lairds kicked up a stink and the cops finally got their arses in gear. They mounted a big operation and caught these clowns from Glasgow shooting deer not that far from here.

'I walked the grounds a few days later and found a rifle in the heather. Beautiful piece of work, a Sako .270, made in Finland, with a Zeiss scope. I reckon one of the poachers threw it away when he tried to make a run for it. He'd probably stolen it in the first place. I didn't see the point of handing it to the cops. It wasn't needed as evidence; the

Glasgow mob had been caught with a van load of carcasses. It would just have been destroyed. That would've been a crying shame, so I kept it.

'I didn't use it for my work, of course. But I'd take it out from time to time and do a bit of target practice with it.'

Alec looked seriously at me.

'I won't be able to do that any more. The rifle's sealed in a waterproof casing and underwater, where it will never be found. Pity, it was a terrific weapon.' He thought for a moment then said, 'But it was worth it. I saw the stuff on the news. All those young lassies, what those evil bastards did to them, forcing them to work in those bloody places.'

The bitch ambled across to us and nuzzled my hand. Alec smiled.

'Twist remembers you. She's a good mother. Looks after her young. And that's what you were doing, Allan. Looking after your wee girl.'

Twist sauntered back to her pups.

'No matter, I still owe you, Alec.'

'No, you don't. A big part of my job is vermin control and that's what that pair were – vermin – and they had to be controlled. When I saw them threatening you, I knew what I had to do, and I'd do it again without giving it a second thought.'

Alec sipped from his mug then said, 'You showed a lot of balls, Allan, facing up to them like that.'

I shook my head.

'Actually, I was shitting myself. I kept thinking, what if something's happened and Alec hasn't made it?'

Alec smiled.

'There was no chance of that. I got there about two hours before they even arrived at the cottage and parked the

Defender about two miles away. I had a good look round and found the perfect spot to cover the front of the cottage, in some bushes under a stand of trees. I reckon the range was about two hundred yards.'

I whistled softly. That seemed a long way to me. Alec guessed what I was thinking.

'With the Sako and that scope I could hardly miss,' he said. 'I watched you walk away, then I picked up the two ejected shells and headed back to the Defender. I was careful. I stuck to the back roads all the way past Dunkeld. I doubt if I passed two cars till I reached Aberfeldy.'

We had finished our tea and we stood up.

'Well, I'd better be getting back,' I said. 'I've booked a table at a very good Italian restaurant in Dundee. There will be four of us. I think it'll be a good night.'

We shook hands and I got in my car and drove away.

Oh, I forgot to mention. I was still seeing Dani and I had been right. She had meant what I thought she meant that first night as I left her flat. Buddy's voice came through the speakers. It was probably a coincidence, but he was singing 'Oh, Boy'.

Acknowledgements

Writing a novel isn't easy, but I found it enjoyable and hugely satisfying. Getting it published brings its own challenges and isn't particularly enjoyable. So, many thanks to my fellow crime-fiction fan, Martin Lindsay, for his help in persuading the people at Black & White to consider *Vermin* worthy of publication.

Thanks, too, to my editor, Rosie Pierce, for her enthusiasm and thoughtful guidance. She made that part fun!